Larry Lunsford

This book is a work of fiction. Any references to historical events, real people, or real locales are used fictitiously. Other names, characters, places, and incidents are products of the author's imagination, and any resemblance to actual events or locales or persons living or dead, is entirely coincidental.

ACKNOWLEDGMENTS

One of my best friends in elementary school was Tim Greenstreet. We shared the hobby of collecting comic books and building models. We traded comics, and I still have a few with his handwritten *Tim* on the cover. We also shared an interest in becoming writers, and one day in early 1967 while visiting at his house, we decided to write a story about a poltergeist. Tim moved to Connecticut and we never wrote anything together. I credit him for giving the writing bug to me.

A big thank you to fraternity brothers Lou Quinto and Mark Francis for taking time from their busy schedules to read the first draft and give valuable feedback. It was difficult for them to be honest because of our close friendship, but they came through with critical and helpful advice. Mark also read a final draft and made invaluable suggestions to improve the novel. He is an amazing editor. Phi phi.

My former student, Achilles Yeldell, also a fraternity brother, and author of the book, *Raised by the Bar*, offered invaluable advice regarding publishing and editing, and designed the book cover. He also graciously proofread the final draft and arranged for his friend, Nate Detweiler, to do the same. I don't know Nate and am deeply appreciative for his helpful suggestions. I am eternally grateful for their assistance.

Another proofreader was Dr. Tony Delgado, a former student, colleague, and an excellent writer. He is making a difference in the lives of university students, and he makes me proud.

As a retired college administrator and assistant professor, there is no greater honor than to see students succeed and excel following graduation. Achilles, Mark, and Tony are among many.

I am grateful to Julio Coto and Cristy Calderón Coto for reviewing the Costa Rica segment as well as checking the Spanish I used in the Tijuana section. We three are members of the esteemed CRaBs (Costa Rica alternative Break) team.

Pura Vida!

For Joan, Megan, and Sean
the loves of my life

Nothing Gold Can Stay

**Nature's first green is gold,
Her hardest hue to hold.
Her early leaf's a flower;
But only so an hour.
Then leaf subsides to leaf.
So Eden sank to grief,
So dawn goes down to day.
Nothing gold can stay.
-Robert Frost
**

1

I am Steve Jackson.

Brad Erickson taught the facts of life to me. I was with him when I smoked my first cigarette. We spent much of our youth together. After several troubling incidences, my parents preferred we go our separate ways, but we didn't. He was my best friend.

Brad and his family moved into the vacant house across the street from me in the Summer of 1963 when I was eleven. He and his family moved to Knoxville from Iowa. The only thing I knew about Iowa was that it is one of the fifty states. A vacationing relative once sent a postcard from Iowa to us, and on the front of the card was a picture of a tractor pulling an ear of corn twice the size of the tractor. I couldn't locate Iowa on a map, but I was anxious to meet someone from there. I had little excitement in my life. My few thrills included buying a new issue of a Gold Key comic book and being allowed to stay up past my bedtime to watch *Candid Camera* on television.

The first thing that excited me was that Brad and I were practically the same age. He was a year older but had started school a year late. We were assigned the same sixth grade class when school started in the Fall.

When I reminisce about those years, I am not happy to admit how naive I was. I found Brad to be knowledgeable about everything. He had striking good looks, a stalking hard body, and was an excellent athlete. He didn't have an ounce of body fat. His prized possession was a 1960 Willie Mays Topps baseball card. He liked The Rolling Stones and The Beatles. He was fearless. He cursed. He spat. He knew about sex.

My parents epitomized Ward and June Cleaver from

2

Leave it to Beaver, one of my favorite childhood television shows. Minus the pearl necklace, my mother dressed the part while performing housework during the day. She was a full-time housewife.

My father, wearing the constant tie, worked as an accountant in a large firm in downtown Knoxville. He was 46 when I was born, and we didn't have a close relationship. We rarely did anything together, and he never taught me to play a sport. His favorite pastime was sitting in his recliner reading the newspaper or a book or watching television. I always believed I wasn't a planned pregnancy.

I had one sister, Janie. She was ten years my senior and had married the Summer after graduating from nearby Maryville College, where she met her husband, Charles T. Clark. He was a transplanted Californian, whose strict Baptist parents forced him East to attend the small, parochial college at the foot of the Great Smoky Mountains. Considering the age difference, we were never close, but we respected that we were each other's only sibling.

My mother was a nosey, yet knowledgeable neighbor. She kept tabs on the comings and goings of our surrounding neighbors. She was once referred to as the Queen of Sheba by a neighbor with whom she argued with over something trivial. The living room curtains remained open, providing the opportunity for her to spy on the neighborhood. She was passing a window when she saw the Ericksons arrive in their filthy, green and white 1956 Chevrolet Bel Air followed by a huge U-Haul truck. She parked at the window to watch the new neighbors move into their house. The house was vacant for over a year, and we were thrilled when a sold sign appeared in the lawn. The realtor informed us that someone from Iowa bought the house, but he had no additional information about the new owner.

3

"I wonder how many kids they have?" she asked. There were only two children in our family, and she wasn't fond of large families. She was an only child.

"Lillian, you're another Hedda Hopper. Get away from that window," my father chided from the living room, relaxing in his recliner, and reading the newspaper. Mom possessed a habit of ignoring people and comments she didn't like. It bothered her that she didn't have scoop on the new neighbors she could share with others. "I'll bake a cake to take over as soon as they're settled. We can get acquainted, and I'll learn all about them," she said. "Neighbors should be familiar with each other."

Dad ignored her. My curiosity aroused, I approached the window, slightly pulled the curtain to one side, and peeked across our well-groomed lawn for a glance at the new arrivals. It was the middle of Summer, and the grass was deep green due to recent rains. It was my assigned task to mow the lawn every Saturday. Dad fertilized twice a year to maintain its pristine appearance. Mom's bright red rose bushes grew on trellises and lined each side of the driveway's entrance.

"Jeeze, look at the size of that dog!" I bellowed as a huge, gorgeous golden retriever smelled its way along the cherry hedges that created a barrier between our yard and the street.

I glanced toward Mom and saw her expression become tense; her eyes disapprovingly followed the dog. I returned my stare, and the dog hiked its leg and relieved itself on Mom's favorite dogwood tree. I chuckled as she shook her head in disgust.

"He'll crap all over our yard," I laughed. "I bet his poop is bigger than a human's!"

Mom found no humor in my comments and continued to shake her head. She worked tediously with her flowers and took pride in bragging that we had the nicest lawn in the neighborhood. She didn't like dogs, and I immediately sensed a potential conflict. She often complained about neighbors' dogs and cats running loose and doing their business on our lawn. You didn't want to be near my mother when she stepped in poop, particularly since we didn't own pets.

I glanced at the new arrivals and spotted a kid about my size that I later learned was Brad. He strutted out of the car like he owned the world. He and a man I assumed to be his father appeared to argue. The man pointed toward the truck, and Brad put his hands on his hips and shook his head, indicating *no way*. Another man exited the U-Haul, wiping his brow with a handkerchief. It was brutally hot, the temperature and humidity both challenging one hundred. Even from my perch, I saw the men's soaked shirts clinging to their bodies.

The man with Brad retrieved a cigarette from a Marlboro box in his shirt pocket and lit it with a stick match he took from his front pants pocket. I watched him flick the match onto the street. He continued to mouth words, waving his hands in frustration, walking to the rear of the U-Haul, and grasping the door handle. Brad stuck his hands in his pockets and practically crawled to join the two men.

The man with Brad struggled to open the huge truck door, and suddenly it flew to the top. A floor lamp tumbled out. Before it hit the ground, Brad grabbed it like a baton and saved it from a certain destructive fate. He triumphantly pitched it above his head, caught it in his other hand, and twirled it behind his back. He glanced toward our house and discovered he had an audience.

He twirled the lamp again and turned toward us in search of approval. It was the ultimate embarrassment. He spotted us spying and gave a slight grin and saluted with his hand holding the lamp. We quickly withdrew from the window, our heads colliding in the process.

Mom hurried to the kitchen, but I remained paralyzed against the wall, waiting minutes before I dared peek to learn if Brad continued watching.

Dad was the self-appointed chair of the neighborhood welcoming committee and believed it was a good idea for us to offer to help the new neighbors. Normally I would jump at the opportunity because I could see their stuff and meet the new kid, but realizing that Brad caught me watching, I was caught off guard. He might say something about us watching them. I needed to create a reason for our action should he mention it.

"Please, Dad, no," I pleaded.

"What's gotten into you, young man?" he responded. "It's the neighborly thing to do. It's a good way to break the ice and meet them. They probably won't accept our offer to help, but they'll appreciate that we offered."

I was humiliated and didn't offer a reason to stay away. I slowly followed him outside and across the yard to meet the new neighbors. I stood in his shadow, staring at my sneakers, my hands deep in my pockets. I felt the heat streaming from the pavement. The city had repaved the street the previous Summer, and it maintained its dark, fresh color and slight smell of new asphalt.

Dad introduced himself and shook hands with Mr. Erickson. Mr. Erickson politely ground his cigarette into the pavement before shaking hands. The others had gone into their new house. Dad introduced me, and we shook hands. My hand was sweaty from nerves and the heat, and I was humiliated, but he didn't appear to notice.

"Well, little fella, I've got a boy about your age, I reckon," he said. "How old are you?"

"Eleven." I meekly responded.

"Brad just turned twelve. I figured you two to be about

the same age. Here he comes."

My heart raced. I prayed Brad wouldn't say anything about us watching him. He joined us and said, "Hey."

Mr. Erickson introduced us. I quickly wiped my hand on my shorts and shook hands with Brad. There was a moment of awkward silence, and my father renewed his offer to help.

"I appreciate the offer, Stan, but I believe we can handle it ourselves. My brother drove the U-Haul and will help with the big stuff. If we run into a jam, we'll come knocking on your door."

"I'll hold you to it," Dad replied. With a quick comment that he was glad to meet them and an invitation to a future barbecue, Dad returned home. "Don't get in the way," he called to me.

I stood in silence, not sure what to say or do. Dad's sudden departure caught me off-guard. "What grade are you in?" Brad asked. I was relieved he broke the ice.

"Sixth," I replied, kicking at small stones in the street.

"Me, too. I started kindergarten a year late, so I'm a year older," he appeared to boast.

"Maybe we'll be in the same class. They have only two sixth grade classes at my school. It's called Central View. It's close enough to walk or ride bikes. Do you have a bike?"

"Yeah, it's in the truck," he pointed toward the U-Haul.

"That'd be neat. I hope we are. Do you like baseball?"

I wasn't much of an athlete but didn't want to admit it to my new friend. "Yeah, a little. Who's your favorite team?"

"The Yankees. They're boss." He flipped a finger against his baseball cap bearing a large NY.

"I like 'em, too," I said.

There was a brief silence. I searched for conversation. "What's your dog's name?"

"Star."

"She's beautiful. How old is she?"

"*He*'s eight," he said, noticeably correcting me.

"We don't have any pets. My mom's not fond of animals," I responded, hoping he'd take note of my response and keep Star off our lawn.

Brad didn't respond and appeared bored, but I continued, "I build model cars and model monsters and collect comic books."

"Monsters?" Brad questioned with a smirk.

"Yeah, you know, like King Kong, Dracula, Godzilla, Superman, The Hunchback of Notre Dame. Come over, and I'll show them to you. They're pretty neat."

Brad didn't appear impressed and probably didn't want to embarrass me. "Maybe later," he said and added, "I have to help move this stuff into the house or my old man will shit."

He cursed. It caught my attention, and I looked at him and smiled. Why was I impressed that he said *shit*? He was nonchalant about it. It came out naturally in his conversation. I couldn't believe it. Talk about being comfortable with someone you just met. This was the beginning of a good relationship.

"Yeah, shit," I responded, and blushed. *Why had I said "shit"?* I am a dork. It was time to leave. I turned and sprinted toward home, calling, "Catch you later." I didn't hear a reply.

2

Thus began a long and not-always-cordial relationship. We were close friends during most of our youth; yet, there were times when our hatred was immense. Our friendship resembled a seesaw. It was up and down. We constantly argued, which was typical of boys our age. It was rarely serious. We had one fist fight, which I lost and suffered a bloody nose. We got along well for long periods and then argued over something trivial such as a game of marbles and refused to speak to each other for days. Our arguments didn't last long, and we'd get back together and pretend nothing happened. Our friendship was puzzling.

That Fall Brad and I were in Mr. Kyker's sixth grade class. He was the first male teacher hired in our elementary school, and I and some of my classmates were afraid of him.

The first day of class was the day after Labor Day. The local municipal pool and parks closed until next Summer. The classroom was spotless and smelled strongly of the newly varnished floors. Mr. Kyker had written his name on the chalk board in large letters. He placed various historical pictures along the walls. I presumed he'd inform us later of their significance to him. One was a picture of President Kennedy. Within two months, it would be graced with a black border. Another was the legendary University of Alabama coach, Bear Bryant. I wondered if Mr. Kyker had attended Alabama.

I caught myself staring at Mr. Kyker's belt. It was dark brown, wide, and appeared to be thick and hard. Corporal punishment was permissible, and I pitied anyone who was whipped with that belt; however, a belt was never used. Mr. Kyker's weapon of choice was a clip board to administer punishment, which normally occurred in gym class. He didn't paddle a student in front of other students in class but took the offender into the equipment storage room and made the student bend and grab his ankles. He'd slap the kid's butt hard with the clip board several times. He left the door open so he wouldn't be inside the room alone with the student. The rest of the class remained completely silent so we could hear the splat of the clip board contact the student's butt. Once we heard the noise, there was a collective "oooooo" from the students. The punished student returned to gym class, head bowed, avoiding the sympathetic stares of classmates.

One afternoon in recess, four of us were playing four square. Chip Fowler accused Benny Rogers of cheating, and Benny took the rubber ball and threw it hard against Chip. Chip retaliated and threw the ball, missed Benny, and hit me in the face. My face stung and turned red. I grabbed the ball and threw it at Chip, but barely missed and hit Patsy Anderson, who wasn't playing with us, in the back of the head. She screamed, attracting Mr. Kyker's attention. He blew his whistle and joined us. "That's enough boys," he said. "Sit on the steps the remainder of recess, and I'll meet you in the equipment room tomorrow in gym class."

It was a totally humiliating experience for me. Not only did my classmates know my pending fate, I had to live with the fact for another day until the punishment was administered.

Girls were never paddled. David Tyson bragged that Mr. Kyker broke his clip board on his butt. If an award were given for the most paddled kid in our class, David would have won.

I attended school with most of the kids in my class since kindergarten, and my social status with them was established. Brad was the new kid on the block and had to prove himself. His self-confidence, good looks, and athletic ability quickly made him popular. Several girls wanted to be his girlfriend, and he became friends with the guys that comprised the *in crowd*. I didn't belong to that group, and I was jealous of the attention Brad received; yet, our friendship survived. Had we not been neighbors, it would have gone in a different direction.

My social standing was elevated because of our friendship. My interests went from building models, reading comic books, and playing Monopoly to shooting hoops and throwing a baseball or football with Brad. His influence was good and bad.

Brad became my protector from sixth grade through high school. I'm not sure why he defended me, but I guess that's what best friends do. The first occurrence I remember was on the playground during recess. It was the second incident that occurred while I played four square. It was my turn to serve from the fourth square after its occupant was ousted. As I moved toward the square, holding the ball, Hugh Pickle grabbed the ball from my grasp and took the fourth square.

Grossly overweight and sporting an outbreak of pimples, he was the class bully. He reeked of urine and bad breath, and our classmates stayed out of his way. His nickname was Dill, but no one dared call him that to his face.

"What the hell," I screamed at him.

"Want to do something about it?" he responded, holding the ball in both hands, and threatening to thrust it at my face.

"It's not your turn, Dill." I quickly realized my error.

"What did you call me, fart breath?"

I couldn't back down in front of my peers and replied, "You heard me."

"Take it back." His voice raised as he wanted to humiliate me in front of as many classmates as possible. The fear of being paddled by Mr. Kyker didn't bother him. He wore it as a badge of honor.

"Screw you and the horse you rode in on," I said, realizing my silly comment.

His next move was fast and furious. He pulled the ball to his chest and was ready to thrust it at me. At the moment he released the ball, Brad appeared and knocked the ball away.

"What the fuck?" Hugh yelled. He was caught off-guard. He paused, unsure if he wanted to confront Brad, yet aware he couldn't back down in front of everyone.

Brad stood his ground, and a staring contest ensued. Who would make the next move?

The whistle blew, ending recess and giving the three of us an escape from the situation. Brad and I walked away, leaving Hugh alone in the fourth square.

"I'm not through with you, Erickson," he screamed.

"I'm really afraid," Brad responded, shooting Hugh his middle finger behind his back.

Brad and I didn't say anything. I didn't thank him because I didn't want him to believe I couldn't have handled the situation, but we both knew Hugh could've beat the shit out of me.

Later in life, I realized that this wasn't the only time Brad came to my rescue.

3

Brad and I lived close to school, and safely walked to and from there without fear of being kidnapped. We usually rode our bikes and parked them in racks on the school grounds and never locked them. I don't remember anyone using bike locks. Who would steal a kid's bicycle? I received a new Schwinn Stingray banana seat bicycle for my birthday. It was the newest bicycle style because of the long, sloped seat, and I was the envy of my schoolmates.

The most memorable day of our young lives occurred later that Fall on November 22. It was unusually warm, Indian Summer weather. We returned to Mr. Kyker's classroom from Miss Smith's music class. I liked music class because we not only sang, we played various instruments. I was in the choir and sang a solo at the Christmas concert in the gymnasium, which had a stage.

The boys in the class believed Miss Smith was *hot*. She was young, pretty, and dressed in the latest fashions. I saw her once in Cas Walker's Supermarket and was amazed that my teacher was there. I am not sure why I found that to be odd, but it was like spotting a celebrity in public. I failed to realize that teachers are human, too, and eat food like the rest of us.

My father bought a used Banner Gibson Archtop guitar in the late 1940s, and he occasionally played. Aside from reading, he had few interests. I was surprised that he played the guitar. I asked him how he learned to play, and he replied that he taught himself. I planned to learn to play, but my musical interest ended with elementary school.

It was near the end of the day, and we were anxious for the final bell to sound. It was Friday, and the weekend awaited us. Our school was not air conditioned, and the huge windows were open in the classroom. The door to the outside playground was propped open. There was no breeze, and even though it was late November, the air was stagnant. Mr. Kyker awaited the bell and allowed the loud discussions to continue. His head rested in his hands, propped on his desk.

Miss Davis was our principal. We believed her to be at least 100 years old. She was an old maid former schoolteacher who had been around forever. She was principal when my older sister attended Central View years earlier. She entered our classroom, glasses propped on top of her head, her hand clutching a handkerchief, and asked for our attention. "Children, I have bad news," she spoke slowly, her voice cracking. "President Kennedy was shot and killed this afternoon in Dallas."

There was an audible gasp. Mr. Kyker shouted, "What?"

We were stunned, and several classmates began to cry. The news brought fear. It was a period when we practiced civil defense exercises. We were accustomed to civil defense sirens routinely sounding since Knoxville bordered Oak Ridge, the Atomic City. Oak Ridge was rumored to be on Russia's list of top ten American cities to bomb because of its nuclear weapons production. The two nuclear bombs dropped on Japan in World War II were partially manufactured there.

Relations were strained between the United States and Russia following the Cuban Missile Crisis and the bungled Bay of Pigs invasion, and we practiced hiding under our desks in case of a nuclear attack. That practice was ludicrous because if a bomb was dropped on Oak Ridge, our school and everything within twenty-five miles would vaporize.

I glanced at the picture of President Kennedy on the wall. My eyes watered. Students were dazed, crying, and unsure what to do. Miss Davis left to inform other classes before the dismissal bell rang, and Mr. Kyker attempted to calm the class. The bell rang, but no one moved. Normally we would have run from the room at the sound of the bell, but we sat in silence except for a few sniffles. Mr. Kyker told us that we could leave and to be calm. "Pray for President Kennedy and his family," he said as we slowly filed out of the room.

Brad and I walked to the intersection adjacent to school, and I spotted my father driving along the sidewalk. Buses stood like frozen monuments, waiting for the little passengers to board. Students wandered like dazed zombies, and teachers attempted to direct students to their destinations. Many parents, like my dad, came to gather their children and take them safely home. An element of fear existed, and it dominated the atmosphere.

My dad stopped and motioned for us to join him. There was total silence as we drove home, except for the car radio providing news reports about the assassination. We pulled into our driveway, and Brad said thanks, jumped out, and jogged home. I entered the house in search of my mother. I sought comfort and reassurance. I located her preparing dinner while softly weeping in the kitchen. She glanced at me and shook her head. Should we hug? It seemed awkward, and I went to my room.

Two days later, Lee Harvey Oswald, the president's alleged assassin, was gunned down by Jack Ruby at police headquarters in Dallas. Could the situation get worse? His death contributed to conspiracy theories, and whether Oswald acted alone or not would never be absolutely determined.

President Johnson declared the following Monday a national day of mourning, and school was canceled. Brad and I were members of the safety patrol, considered a cool thing, along with being a Junior Fire Marshall, and we had the honor of raising the flag daily at school. For 30 days, we raised the flag and lowered it to half-mast. On the first day, Miss Davis taught us how to perform the task; otherwise, we would have raised it to half-mast and left it instead of taking it to the top first and lowering it.

I was too young to know much about the Kennedy administration and whether to appreciate it. I simply realized that something tragic occurred, and the world was sad, although some school children in Texas allegedly applauded when they heard the news. It was the worst thing that had occurred in my young life, and it is one of the days that I will never forget.

We watched the funeral on our black and white television. I remember President Kennedy's young three-year-old son, John, Jr., saluting the caisson carrying his father's casket, which was followed by a riderless horse, boots turned backward in the stirrups. I collected newspaper and magazine articles about the assassination and compiled a huge folder of materials. Many years later in my newspaper career, I wrote articles detailing my memories of the President's death on the twentieth and twenty-fifth anniversaries of the event.

Brad didn't appear phased by President Kennedy's death. He was upset about his favorite television programs being preempted by coverage of the assassination and funeral. He was happy-go-lucky and had little concern for matters outside his narcissistic, intimate world.

Sixth grade was an age of presumed innocence. A false sense of security existed. It ended abruptly on November 22, 1963.

4

One of our older friends, Sam Dirksen, the first truly bad person I knew, had a clubhouse behind his home on the next street. His father built the small building as a workshop but later converted part of his garage into his workshop and gave the small building to Sam for a playhouse. Sam didn't call it a playhouse because that was too juvenile. The building was windowless except for a six-inch opening covered by wire screen around the top. It was too high to see in or out but allowed air to flow through on hot days. His father ran electricity from the house so that it could have a light and small fan. It had a lock on the inside of the door so no one could enter when it was occupied unless allowed inside. It was a gathering place for us to play cards or games, to talk and brag, but mainly to get away from adults. Sam and his friends were older, and I learned much from them.

My parents considered Sam a hood, and I was told to keep my distance. He was known to be the neighborhood bully, and I didn't want to get on his bad side. I wasn't sure if the stories I'd heard were true or embellished to increase his reputation. He allegedly shot birds and squirrels with a BB gun. I heard he carried a switch blade and cut several guys in fights. There were various rumors about the origin of the scar on his cheek. He had a Honda 150 motorcycle and allegedly belonged to a gang. I wouldn't have strayed into his territory had Brad not coerced me into going to the clubhouse the first time.

My parents would have been angry and would have forbidden me to hang with Sam had they known I was doing just that. Everything I learned in Sam's clubhouse wasn't good. It was there in the Summer of 1964 before I started junior high school and the seventh grade that I smoked my first cigarette. Several vulgar words were also added to my vocabulary.

17

Brad claimed that he had been smoking since he was ten, but I didn't believe him. He once pulled a pack of cigarettes out of the front of his underwear when we walked through the woods on the way to the community swimming pool or the Boys' Club and lit one. Even though he never ceased to amaze me, I was surprised when he pulled a pack of Winstons from his underwear. He offered one, and I refused, acknowledging that my parents would smell cigarette smoke on me a mile away. Rather than admit that I'd never smoked, I said that I was not going to touch something that had been in his underwear. He smiled and laughed but offered no retort.

We decided to stop by Sam's clubhouse one afternoon to see if anyone was there. We knocked on the door, and it opened slightly, and one of Sam's friends peeked out. I heard hm say, "It's the kids." Sam had a chin-up bar, and Brad and I entered, and sat on the bar. Three other guys were there, and when they accepted a cigarette from Sam, I caved to the peer pressure and took one when the pack was passed to me.

"Hey, the virgin gives in!" Brad quipped.

"Shut up and give me a match," I replied.

"My face and your ass!" he said, and everyone laughed.

I watched the others light their cigarettes so that I appeared I knew how when it was my turn. I struck the wooden match too hard and broke the tip. I removed another one and gently struck it. I watched the flame settle and slowly brought the match to the cigarette hanging from my lips. My hand quivered, and I suspected that my friends were watching and silently laughing.

I inhaled too deeply and gagged on the smoke. I coughed and spat the smoke from my burning lungs. Brad and the others laughed, and he pounded me on the back, making it worse.

"I thought you were a veteran smoker," Brad said.

I pushed his hand away, scolding, "Will you stop, asshole!"

"Just trying to help. Don't want you choking to death. I'll let you die before I'll give you CPR."

The others laughed, and my cheeks flushed.

"I'd rather die than let you," I said, and realized it was a stupid response.

Sam shook his head.

I pretended to inhale and let the cigarette burn and put it out as soon as possible. I smiled proudly, believing I passed the test. Each cigarette I accepted in the future became easier, although I smoked only with Brad.

5

At first, my parents were pleased that we became friends, but began to question the amount of influence Brad had on me. He played a vital role in my maturation process, and I don't believe our friendship created more negative than positive consequences. I learned to make choices, although not necessarily the right ones. I relied less on my parents and looked to Brad for advice and direction.

There was an occasion, however, that led to the first rift in our relationship and caused my parents to pause and question my spending too much time with Brad.

We lived in Knoxville's West Hills, which was desolate until Interstate 40 cut through its center, and West Town Mall opened when I was in college in 1972. Prior to that, dozens of small shopping centers existed along Kingston Pike, the main thoroughfare, and we often rode bikes in the parking lots, bought Slurpees at the new 7-Eleven, and treated ourselves to banana splits at the lunch counter in Woolworth's. Woolworth's charged thirty-nine cents for a banana split. I remember that they once hung balloons above the counter, and in each was a piece of small paper with the price an individual paid for the banana split. The price varied from one cent to the full thirty-nine cents. Who could resist paying a penny for a banana split?

On one visit to Woolworth's, I decided to try my luck at picking the balloon with the penny price hidden inside. I sat on one of the red, rotating stools at the counter and chose a blue balloon, my favorite color. The paper in the balloon contained the full price. That upset me. I was gullible and even though I didn't want or need another banana split, I finished the first one and decided to attempt to pick the balloon with the one cent written on the paper. I selected a bright red balloon, and much to my chagrin, the paper read thirty-five cents. I angrily paid the amount and forcibly ate the second banana split. I challenged the counter server if any balloons truly held papers with a penny or less than twenty cents on them. She replied, "Yes, honey. I saw them write the numbers on 'em myself." I didn't explain to my mother why I wasn't hungry at supper that evening.

Woolworth's was a cool hangout. They had a tremendous toy department with plastic model kits containing every imaginable model car, airplane, and monster. Each kit had parts and instructions for gluing the pieces. Once completed, the model was painted to match the one featured on the cover of the box. Small bottles of various paint colors, tubes of glue, and paint brushes were sold. One Summer they sponsored a monster model contest. I entered my Hunchback of Notre Dame and Wolfman models. I meticulously painted both, which were displayed along with the other entrants in the store's front window. I considered my Wolfman to be the best and assumed I'd win first place; however, neither of my models placed in the contest. I was disappointed and accused the judges of cheating.

Another section of the store had a spinning rack stocked with the latest comic books, whose cost had recently gone from a dime to twelve cents each. My favorite brand was Gold Key. Another classmate, Tommy Bailey, collected comics, and we often traded once we read our new purchases.

There was a pet department, where we pestered the birds, fish, white mice, hamsters, and tiny turtles until a store clerk asked us to leave them alone.

Easter was a fun time because they sold different colored baby chicks that were housed under blazing hot lights. I didn't know it, but they were often diseased, and the one time I bought one, it died that same night. I cried and buried it by the fence in the back yard. I had a similar experience with a hamster. It was dead by the end of the week, which was my fault. I dropped it on its head on the concrete sidewalk, quickly ending its short life. I cried and buried it adjacent to the baby chick. My goldfish was also buried in my growing makeshift cemetery. My parents wanted to flush the fish down the toilet, but I refused.

It was a hot Summer day when Brad called and asked if I wanted to ride to the Pike and buy a Slurpee. I was playing with toy cars and building roads with my marble collection on the living room carpet and accepted the chance to get out of the house.

"Sure," I said. "I'll meet you in the street."

We raced most of the way to 7-Eleven, with Brad finishing far ahead. We were hot and thirsty from the ride, and we downed the drinks too quickly and our throats burned from the chill of the flavored ice. I suffered a brain freeze and cringed from the pain. It hurt as much as getting kicked in the balls.

"Let's see if they have snakes at Woolworth's," Brad said, pitching his empty cup and straw on the sidewalk.

"Don't litter," I scolded.

"Hey, they're young. They'll get over it. Besides, it creates a job for someone so that they won't have to be on welfare."

"Sarcastic bastard," I laughed, pitched my cup and straw into a waste basket, and mounted my bike.

Brad was out of hearing distance and shouting, "I'll race you," over his shoulder as he sped across the parking lot. I hurried to catch him, knowing my effort was in vain.

After intimidating the fish and being chased from harassing the birds by a store clerk, Brad and I sauntered to the models. Brad wasn't into models, and my interest was waning, but I wanted to see if any new ones were added to the shelves.

22

"Wow! Look at this '58 T-bird. It's really boss," Brad exclaimed.

I glanced at the box and agreed, but a new Superman model caught my eyes. The cover of the model's box featured the man of steel breaking through a red brick wall. I scanned the shelf in search of monster models I didn't have but spotted only the Superman model. I decided to buy it later.

The model planes caught Brad's attention, and he viewed the box covers of several types of planes. He lifted a World War II B-17 Flying Fortress model plane box from the shelf and stared at the picture.

"I've always wanted to fly," he said. "My dream is to skydive. That would be an amazing experience, and such a free feeling falling from the plane to the ground."

"No way, man," I replied. "You couldn't pay me a million dollars to jump out of a plane. I hate heights. I'd have a heart attack and never pull the rip cord." He replaced the model plane and picked up a model car box. "Man, this car is really boss. I can't wait to get my license and buy an old car to restore. God, T-birds cost a mint." He stared at the box.

"Yeah," I agreed, "that jerk Charlie Cunningham on Wallingford Drive has one. He rarely drives it. Just washes and polishes it every damn weekend," I replied. "It's such a waste for it to sit in his driveway all the time and not be driven. I wish it were mine. I'd take it out every day."

I replaced the Superman model and selected a box containing a model of The Creature.

"Hey, man, I've got to piss like a wild racehorse. I'll go bleed the lizard and meet you at the bikes," Brad exclaimed.

"Okay," I said, and headed to the comics as he turned toward the restroom and the store's rear. I wanted to take a quick glance at the new Gold Key issues without Brad knowing. I didn't want to be seen looking at models and comics in the same day. I was growing out of both, but not quite yet.

I didn't spend much time glancing at the comics because I knew it wouldn't take long for Brad to pee. I waited impatiently outside the store and decided that Brad was purposely stalling because he knew I had to be home in time for supper.

Ten minutes passed, and I became more restless. I needed to return home because my mother didn't like anyone to be late for supper. I spat on a large red ant, trying to drown it, until I ran out of saliva.

Sighing a quiet, "damn", I dismounted, engaged the kick stand, and reentered the store to locate Brad. As I slowly walked the store's front, glancing down the aisles, I spotted Brad in the aisle with the models.

He was standing with two store employees, and from appearances, I determined that he was involved in a heated exchange. The employees pointed fingers. Brad waved his hands and shook his head.

I increased my pace and joined them to learn the problem.

"What's up?" I asked.

I was ignored. The two employees glanced at me with annoyance, and believing that I was a nosey kid, returned to their confrontation with Brad. Brad stole a glance in my direction but quickly turned his head toward the floor.

I asked louder, "What's up?"

One of the employees I presumed was the manager because he was dressed in a shirt and tie, turned, and rudely responded, "Are you with this young man?"

I quickly nodded.

"Maybe he's got something, too," the other employee said.

"What's wrong, Brad?" I demanded.

"They accused me of shoplifting." He briefly glanced at me and bowed his head.

"He had this under his shirt"" the clerk said, holding up the model Thunderbird box.

Silence.

"Ah, crap," I said, kicking the floor with my sneaker.

"I was going to pay for it," blurted Brad. "You didn't give me the chance to go to the cash register."

"Yeah, and the Pope ain't Catholic," the young clerk smartly replied.

"Young man, you need to come with us to the office," the manager took Brad by the arm. Brad jerked away.

"Don't make this more difficult than it already is," the manager insisted.

I wanted to help. My heart raced. My stomach churned. I almost threw up. My imagination ran wild, and I considered the worst: the manager calling the cops and Brad taken away in handcuffs. I imagined him holding jail bars, dressed in a striped prisoner's uniform.

"Jesus, Brad," I said without reason.

I was desperate and pleaded, "Look, I'll pay for the model car. Please let him go." I removed my Roy Rogers wallet from my rear pocket.

"Sorry, son. He should have known better. It's thieves like him that cause other people to pay higher prices because we have to raise them to recoup losses from shoplifters," the manager insisted.

He took Brad by the arm and the three walked toward the store's office. Brad avoided eye contact with me. I wondered if I would see him again. My eyes followed the three until they disappeared. As he was led away, he resembled a condemned prisoner making his way to the gas chamber. It was a scene from *The Twilight Zone*.

My eyes watered, and I wanted to leave before I cried. I sprinted to my bike. I saw Brad's bike and pondered what would happen to it. I couldn't push two bikes home. I concluded that it wasn't my problem. A larger problem existed.

I sped home. I don't remember crossing Kingston Pike, and I'm amazed I wasn't hit and killed by a car. I reached home and was out of breath. I bent my body, resting my hands on my knees to catch my wind.

My thoughts continued to run wild. "Damn, what am I going to do? Should I tell Mom and Dad what happened?" I said with petrified anxiety. I knew they would be angry and question the role I played in the incident.

I quietly tiptoed into the house and slipped to my room undetected and quietly closed the door. I lay on my bed with my hands under my head, staring blankly at the ceiling.

I was lucky to have a small stereo that I bought for $60 at J.C. Penney's from Christmas money and funds I'd saved from my paper route. I had a small album collection. A British group, The Beatles had taken over the American music scene. I bought their second album released in the U. S., *Meet the Beatles*. I also liked Motown records and bought the new album by the hot Motown group, The Supremes. One of my favorite groups was The Animals, and I constantly played their version of *House of the Rising Sun*. My favorite was another newcomer, Bob Dylan. He was a rebel, and when I turned twelve, conflicts with my parents increased and I, too, began to rebel.

I put on the Dylan album, *The Freewheelin' Bob Dylan,* and placed the needle on the track, *Blowin' in the Wind*. So many questions in my young mind. Why did Brad steal the model car? It made no sense. Were we still friends? Is he grounded for life?

The answer, my friend, is blowin' in the wind. The answer is blowin' in the wind.

I fell asleep.

I was startled awake by the ringing of the telephone. I glanced at my clock. It was almost 5:00. Dad would arrive from work in half an hour. I decided to remain in my room until supper, although I had to pee, badly. The record reached the end of the last song, and the sound of the needle continuously scratching filled the room. I turned off the stereo because I wanted to hear when my father arrived home. I needed to prepare a response to their imminent interrogation.

My ears became sensitive listening devices. My father's arrival was announced by the garage door opening exactly at 5:45. The door mechanism was old and rusted and rattled the entire house when operating.

I waited impatiently for fifteen minutes. Did they know or not? Death would have been welcomed compared to the waiting. The knock broke the silence.

My parents entered my room while still knocking.

"Steve, I believe we have something to talk about, don't we?" Dad asked.

They remained standing, donning unforgiving cold, hard stares. My mother dabbed her eyes with a tissue. I didn't respond.

The silence was deadening. My father spoke again, "I understand you and Brad had some trouble at Woolworth's today."

"It wasn't me," I shot back.

"That remains to be seen, young man," he replied. My mother dabbed her eyes again.

Their standing was their method of asserting authority. I had done nothing wrong, and I refused to be implicated in the incident.

I continued my defense, "I didn't know he took something."

"How could he stuff a model car box down the front of his shirt and you not see?" Dad asked.

My anger grew because I was being accused of being an accessory to a crime, and I didn't appreciate it. Other than occasionally being a smart-ass, I was a good son, never getting into trouble. I couldn't remember a time when they were disappointed in me.

"I wasn't with him when he did it," I shouted. I reviewed the entire scenario for them and heaved a huge sigh in disgust. I refused to cry.

I believe they finally realized that they overreacted and were hopefully ashamed by their abrupt confrontation with me.

"How did you find out?" I asked, breaking the quiet.

"Mrs. Erickson called," my mother said, dabbing her eyes.

"Is Brad in jail?" I asked.

"No, he's home. They called his father at work to come to the store," Dad said. "How embarrassing," he continued. "I just can't fathom it. A stupid model car. He's lucky they didn't call the police. He'd have a record, and his name would be in the *News Sentinel*."

"They don't print juveniles' names," I smartly countered.

"Watch your mouth, young man, or you'll be grounded, too," Dad shot back.

"Is Brad grounded?" I asked.

"What do you think? Of course he is. And you're not allowed to see him until we say so, and both of you are permanently banned from Woolworth's," Dad said, loosening his tie and adjusting his pants on his growing waist.

I was angry, and I sat on the side of my bed to gain a better position in my arguing power.

"Why am I being punished? I told you I didn't do

anything. Why can't I see Brad? And who banned me from Woolworth's, you, or them? I wouldn't go back there if you gave me a million dollars."

"We don't intend to stand here the entire evening arguing with you. You heard what we said, and we don't want to hear anything else about it. Get ready for supper," Dad was finished, and he and Mom exited, Mom taking one last dab at her eyes.

"Screw you," I said to myself. I was pissed. Royally pissed, whatever that meant.

I pouted in my room for three or four days, refusing to exit except for supper and to mow the lawn. I hoped I was upsetting my parents with my behavior, but they didn't care.

Brad called the next day when he was aware that my parents weren't home.

"I thought you are grounded," I said.

"I am, but Mom went to the store. I'm bored as hell. What did your folks say?"

"They accused me of being involved, too. I was pissed. I can't believe you did something so stupid. Why did you do it?"

"I was framed."

"Yeah, right. Dip shit."

"Anyway, I don't want to talk about it anymore. Hey, would you buy a pack of cigarettes for me? I'm dying for a butt."

"No. No way. You already got me in enough trouble, you jerk."

"Come on. Be a pal. I'd do it for you."

"I said no."

"Some friend you are." He hung up the phone.

I considered calling and hanging up when he answered but didn't. I knew he wasn't mad. He probably assumed I'd call immediately and offer to buy the cigarettes, but no way. No way. No way.

"Hello," Brad answered slowly and politely.

"Alright, asshole, I'll get them. If I get into trouble, that's it. We're through."

"You're a true pal!"

Jeeze, I couldn't believe that I gave in. It required riding my bike across Kingston Pike to the Shell service station and buying the cigarettes from a machine. I couldn't go to 7-Eleven because they wouldn't sell to a minor. I prayed a neighbor wouldn't see me purchase the cigarettes and tell my parents. God, I was gullible!

My errand went without problems. I stuffed the pack of Winstons down the front of my underwear because that's what Brad did, and I wanted him to be grossed out when I pulled them from my underwear. I wished I hadn't done it because when I pedaled, the cigarette pack rubbed my penis and it hurt like hell. The things we do for friends.

Luckily, Mrs. Erickson's car was gone when I returned, and I risked the trip to Brad's house to give the cigarettes to him. He opened the door before I knocked and took the cigarettes from my hand.

"You owe me big time," I said.

"Thanks, man, you're a true friend. You'd better go before my mother gets home. She'll be back any minute, and I'll be up shit creek if she finds you here." He grabbed the pack and closed the door. I was hoping for a longer conversation, but his action ended that thought.

"What about my fifty cents?" I yelled. The door didn't open, and my knocking was in vain. I didn't want to get caught, so I returned home, cursing myself and Brad.

6

As quickly as the seasons changed in our young lives, the Woolworth's incident disappeared. Another Fall arrived, and with it, a new school year. One of the highlights of every September during my youth was the annual Tennessee Valley Fair held at Knoxville's Tennessee Fair Grounds. Mom usually took me unless I accompanied a friend and his or her parents. September 1964, Mom and Mrs. Erickson took Brad and me. It was Brad's first Tennessee Valley Fair, and I knew he was in for the time of his life. I was glad that he was going so I had someone to take the rides and play the various carnival games with.

As soon as we entered the gates, Brad and I played games, attempting to win cheap prizes. Most of the games were rigged, and considering the money we spent, we could have bought the prizes cheaper at Woolworth's. We rode several rides, and I needed a break when I became nauseated on the roller coaster. We stuffed ourselves on elephant ears, grilled corn-on-the-cob, and turkey legs.

I recognized the sound of basketballs hitting rims, and we walked toward the sound. Brad found a game he could win. For a dollar, we had to make three baskets with three attempts. The prize was a huge stuffed animal of our choice. Four hoops were attached to a huge wooden wall several feet from the shooting line. It looked impossible to make one shot, much less three. I went first and missed on my first attempt and shot the remaining two baskets for the hell of it. Brad made the first two and missed the third. He cussed and pulled another dollar bill from his pocket. He was two-for-two and stalled, relaxing before attempting his final shot. Others gathered to watch. I didn't say anything because I knew he would tell me to be quiet.

He aimed the ball, flipped it easily from his hand, and

watched it sail through the air. It hit the backboard above the basket. The ball dropped on the steel hoop and made several revolutions before finally dropping through. The bystanders cheered, and I slapped him on the back and told him congratulations, as did his mother and mine. The game attendant said, "Way to go, man," and asked him which stuffed animal he wanted. I don't believe Brad wanted the prize. He wanted only to prove he could make the three consecutive baskets. He chose a huge Teddy bear and immediately handed it to his mother. He was too proud to carry it. His mother didn't want to carry it, but she was aware that he would rather discard it than carry it, so she accepted the burden.

We encountered a station with a carnie standing next to a large scale. A shelf filled with cheap ceramic busts of President John F. Kennedy, a carnival monkey, and a green frog stood behind the scale. The carnie enticed the crowd to allow him to guess their age within two years or their weight within five pounds. I was a skinny little dude for my age and decided to go with guessing my weight. I handed him fifty cents, which he pocketed. He held a small tablet and pen and wrote figures on a page after closely examining me head to toe and asking me to turn around. He told me to stand on the scale, and I watched as the pointer quickly rose and settled on 129 pounds. He asked how old I was, and I responded twelve. He showed the paper to everyone, which read 120 pounds. He was off nine pounds, and I won the prize.

"Right on the nose!" the carnie screamed with pride and stuffed the paper in his pocket.

"No way," I responded. "You were nine pounds off. You wrote 120."

"It said 129. You confused the nine with a zero. Now get lost."

I stood my ground. Mom and Mrs. Erickson were

resting on a bench and didn't notice the confrontation.

"Give him the prize," Brad demanded. Others nodded and sounded agreement.

"I said get lost," the carnie responded. "Who's next?"

"You've got one last chance or I call a cop," Brad retorted.

The carnie hesitated and noticed a growing crowd. "What d'ya want, you little turd?" He pointed toward the shelf.

I picked the Kennedy bust, which he removed from the shelf and thrust into my chest. I considered responding with a nasty or sarcastic comment but decided it was best to leave while I was ahead. I carried the prize for a while and eventually gave it to my mother.

We rode cars through a haunted house, which we found stupid and not scary. Next were the bumper cars. Brad and I spent the entire ride purposely colliding into each other until the attendant cautioned us to stop or be kicked off the ride.

We entered a hall of glass and mirrors. It was more difficult to find our way out than I expected. We continually collided with glass panels. I expected to have a bruised forehead the next day. Brad became angry and wanted out. I told him to relax and continued using my hands to follow the panels. We finally located the exit and breathed a sigh of relief. I jokingly told Brad I wanted to go again, and he replied no way and said I was going alone if I did.

Our last activity before the closing show was visiting the freak house. Mom and Mrs. Erickson refused to go. We bought tickets and entered a facility with several enclosed glass rooms. We walked by each one and witnessed various individuals with disabilities on display. There were Siamese twins, a bearded lady, and other individuals labeled as freaks of nature. It was disgusting, and Brad and I wanted to leave, but we had to make our way past all the windows before we could exit. The last featured individual was a huge man, seven feet tall and weighing several hundred pounds. An employee sold rings engraved with the man's LG initials for twenty-five cents. The ring fit on his ring finger. I bought one, and it fit on all four of my fingers. He was the biggest person I've ever seen.

I wish we hadn't gone into the freak show but were too young to know better. Excluding the freak house, it was a fun and exhausting day and concluded with a show at the outdoor amphitheater featuring actors Max Baer, Jr., Donna Douglas, and Irene Ryan from the television show, *The Beverly Hillbillies*. It was one of my favorite shows. Max played Jethro Bodine, Donna was Elly May Clampett, and Irene was Granny Clampett. The three performed several small skits and shared stories with the audience. I didn't know why Buddy Ebsen, who played Jed Clampett, wasn't there, but wished that he was so that we had seen the entire cast. It was a nice culmination to a long and enjoyable day.

7

The next Fall event which drew my attention was the presidential election. I became consumed with the election between President Lyndon Johnson and Arizona Senator Barry Goldwater. My parents were Democrats, and demonstrative of my rebel ways, I chose to support Goldwater.

The Republican Party opened a campaign office in a small trailer in a shopping mall parking lot on Kingston Pike. I rode my bike there on a Saturday and introduced myself to a woman campaign worker. I informed her I wanted to volunteer for Goldwater. She introduced herself as Cathy and appeared unsure of a response or what to do with me. Following thoughtful consideration, she suggested that I sit at a table filled with campaign materials outside the trailer and allow visitors to take what they wanted. If anyone had questions or inquiries about the campaign, I could summon Cathy.

I quickly placed two Goldwater buttons on my shirt. One read "AuH2O." I didn't understand what that meant and asked Cathy. She explained that "Au" is the symbol for gold on the Periodic Table of the Elements and that H2O is the symbol for water; thus, Goldwater. I loved that pin. I scribbled "LBJ for ex-President" on a piece of paper and put it inside a nametag holder and wore that with my Goldwater buttons. The Democratic Party had a similar trailer at the other end of the shopping center, and I paraded by there a few times, hoping they would see the collection of buttons on my shirt.

One afternoon Cathy introduced me to a young man named Howard Baker, Jr. He was running for the U.S. Senate against incumbent liberal Democrat Ross Bass. Handsome and eloquent, he politely signed a bumper sticker for me, a souvenir I still possess. He lost the election but eventually went on to win and served three terms in the Senate and held several other top political posts, including serving as chief of staff for President Ronald Reagan. He became one of the most powerful politicians in Washington and played an important role in the impeachment hearings against President Nixon during the Watergate scandal.

Sen. Goldwater had an uphill battle in his campaign against President Johnson. The senator lost much support when he suggested that the Tennessee Valley Authority (TVA) be sold to private enterprise. The Democrats issued a double bumper sticker that read "Sell TVA? I'd Rather Sell Arizona." I placed a Goldwater bumper sticker on our family car, a 1959 Ford Ranch Wagon, causing my father to chastise me and order its immediate removal.

My volunteering was limited to Saturdays due to school. I became a sidekick around the office and completed any request. The staff allowed me to tag along to canvass door-to-door to distribute materials and solicit support for Goldwater. It was a tough charge because Knoxville voters traditionally leaned Democratic. That was reinforced when I was bitten by a dog in one neighborhood. It didn't draw blood, so I didn't inform anyone. I assumed my parents would be furious and end my volunteer activities.

The election was November 3, and Goldwater was soundly defeated. I was disappointed but too young to be sorely affected. I enjoyed the experience and exposure to politics and immediately anticipated the 1968 campaign.

I am amazed how naive I was about life until I met Brad. It is difficult to comprehend how a farm boy from Iowa knew much more about the thing that consumed my youthful thoughts---sex! I found my father's hidden *Playboys* in his closet one day while looking for something. I heard jokes about *threading the needle* in gym class at school, but my parents never provided the spill about the birds and the bees.

I don't believe he was fully knowledgeable, but Brad knew more about sex than me. When I was in third grade, I asked my mother where babies come from, and she told me that God plants seeds in women, and they grow into babies. That was good enough for me until Brad and the neighborhood boys filled in the gaps. It was a matter of fact for Brad, and he bragged about going all the way with a girl named Sarah when he lived in Iowa. I begged for the sordid details, but Brad refused, claiming it was private. I knew he had nothing to tell because he would have been too young to have done the dirty deed.

I was full of dreams, though, not only during the day, but at night, too, when occasionally they were wet. I was early into puberty, and there wasn't much mess.

Another Summer ritual was visiting girls at their houses and playing kissing games in their basement, praying a parent wouldn't drop in unexpectedly.

There was hope of copping a feel, and once I was lucky to have a girl *accidentally* rub her elbow on my crotch and feel the growing bulge hidden there. I was new at kissing, and sometimes our teeth would hit. We pretended it didn't happen and offered a slight snicker. God forbid if she had braces! That was the pits!

We also attended parties where board games were replaced by Spin the Bottle and Seven Minutes in Heaven once parents retired to another room for the evening. Seven Minutes in Heaven involved taking the person of the opposite sex on whom the bottle landed into a closet alone for seven minutes. Imaginations ran wild. When it was my time to visit the closet, my partner and I, whose name I can't remember, only chatted, but before returning to the room with the other partiers, I partially unbuttoned and pulled my shirt out of my pants and messed my hair. We received snide comments upon our return, and we blushed, I with pride, she with embarrassment.

Undoubtedly what Brad and I told each other was untruthful, but it was the guy thing to do, and I played along like most boys did and still do at that discovering age.

I struggled to maintain pace with Brad. I read comics and built models. That childhood routine was replaced by going to the Summer playground at our elementary school where we played on the softball team against other school playgrounds.

My father wasn't an athlete and never practiced with or encouraged me to participate in sports. When I joined the playground team, I bought a glove and ball and learned from scratch. Brad helped by teaching the fundamentals and throwing with me. He concluded that since I had not learned to bat, he taught me to bat left-handed. He said there are fewer left-handed batters, and I would get more hits from that side than from the right. I found the game challenging and exciting and became a fair player.

Competition wasn't tough in the playground league because everyone was allowed to play. Our team progressed to the championship game that Summer, where we lost to Riverdale, 12-7. I had two hits, scored a run, and caught a fly ball for an out in my right field position. On one play, a fly ball flew over my head and allowed the batter to reach third base. We made several errors. Brad had a throwing error from his short stop position, which allowed the missed ball over my head to be less embarrassing.

The playground had a full-time staff and was open Monday to Friday from 9 a.m. to 3 p.m. We didn't go every day, but it served as a babysitter for many kids, and Brad and I attended two or three days a week. They had various contests, such as the ugliest pet contest, four square, tetherball, and rolly bat. We also played kickball and Red Rover. Red Rover was later banned due to injuries suffered by kids when their arms were hit by individuals attempting to break through the chain they formed with their hands and arms.

At Summer's end in August, the county's school playgrounds joined to host a circus at Chilhowee Park off Magnolia Avenue in East Knoxville. Our playground built a funny police car with cardboard. Some of us dressed as Keystone Cops, and the remaining kids dressed as clowns. We performed a stunt where over twenty of us exited the police car. As clowns and Keystone Cops, we acted comically and hit each other with foam rubber batons. The crowd howled. Brad said he didn't want to look silly and refused to participate in the circus. Actually, he was just too cool.

....

One of the major challenges came in the ninth grade when we participated in the required Presidential Physical Fitness Test. Considered sadistic and abolished many years later, it became a major goal to prove our physical fitness and win the award. The test consisted of seven physical exercises with minimum standards that must be passed to win the award.

Although I was terrified of the challenge, I was determined to succeed. The seven exercises consisted of pullups, sit-ups, standing broad jump, 50-yard dash, softball throw, shuttle run, and 600-yard run. I was a runner and wasn't concerned about events that involved running; however, I worried about the softball throw. Although I played softball in the Summer playground league, I wasn't sure that sufficed to prepare me to throw the required distance for the test.

The program was administered in May. Brad and I were in the same gym class where the event took place. The pullups, sit-ups, and shuttle run were held over a two-day period due to the size of the class, and each test was individual.

Brad breezed through all three. I didn't have significant arm strength and struggled with the pullups but met the minimum. I experienced a proud moment when I tied the school's sit-up record by completing 98 sit-ups in two minutes. The test required that our feet be held by a partner while completing the sit-ups. Brad was my partner and heartily cheered me through each one. I was happy but upset that time ran out before I could add one more sit-up and break the record.

The standing broad jump, 50-yard dash, softball throw, and 600-yard run took place outside over several days. Realizing that I had difficulty with the pullups, my concern about the softball throw increased. I asked Brad to work with me a few days prior to the test, and we practiced on our home street. We measured the required distance, and I made several attempts but couldn't meet the minimum. Brad was patient and provided several tips, but none worked. He advised me to quit worrying so much about it because it would result in my screwing up on test day. I was disappointed and angry. I passed six of the seven tests, and only the softball throw remained.

Winning the Presidential Physical Fitness Award meant the world to me. I had something to prove to my peers, and pressure was building. I compared the situation to Brad attempting a last-second shot in a basketball game where his team was down by one point. If he made the shot, his team won. If not, they lost. He said it was a good analogy and insisted that I would pass. He remained positive and encouraged me throughout the ordeal.

The final test day arrived, and the gym class met on the football practice field in the center of the track for the softball throw. The boys and girls had separate gym classes. My classmates and I were dressed in the required white gym shorts, white t-shirt, and white tennis shoes. It was a warm day, the sun glaring down on our bare heads. My mouth was dry from being nervous. I wished I had taken a drink from the water fountain before going outside.

Each student had three chances to meet the minimum distance. We were called in alphabetical order, and Brad threw and met the requirement on his first throw. I waited my turn while watching the techniques of the other boys. There were cheers when a student passed and audible sighs when a student failed.

The coach called my name, and I stepped up to the chalk line to attempt my first throw. A cloud covered the field, and I could better see the target line. The minimum throwing distance was marked on the field, and an assistant coach stood ready to measure each throw. I took a deep breath and stared at the target. Brad whispered, "You can do this." I took a wind-up and threw as hard as I could. I followed the ball's path and watched it hit the ground short of the marked goal.

"Shit," I said.

"Second throw," coach said, ignoring my comment. "Take your time. You can do it, Steve. You were only a couple yards short."

I repeated my warm-up routine. I spied the chalk line and aimed the ball. I wasn't nervous the first throw, but my anxiety increased as my classmates stood in silence, their eyes bearing down on me. I rushed the throw and fell short of my first attempt.

"Fuck," I mouthed the word but not aloud.

"Last chance, Steve," coach said. "Shake it off and concentrate."

Brad stepped up and whispered in my ear, "Pretend you're throwing at the person you hate most in the world." I smiled and gave it a thought.

I wiped my wet hand on my gym shorts, took a wind-up, and threw the ball with all my might. I was afraid to look, knowing I might cry, but I watched the ball sail through the air and land a few feet beyond the assistant coach. I heard him yell, "Pass!"

    I jumped with joy. Coach congratulated and slapped me on the back. Brad and other classmates hugged and gave me congratulatory hits on my body. I was a Presidential Physical Fitness Award recipient! Once the certificate arrived, I placed it in a nice frame and hung it on my bedroom wall. It remained there for many years.

    Brad asked later who I pretended to hit with the ball, and I replied, "You!"

8

Junior high school ended, and Brad further solidified his status as the big man on campus. I continued to feel like a tag-along, but I didn't mind because I depended on Brad when I needed help, and he undoubtedly relied on, and used me.

As an adult, when I meet high school students, I'm amazed how young they appear, and realize they *are* young. Yet, when I was in high school, I considered myself an adult and believed I knew everything. We were cocky and invincible.

Brad was a natural-born athlete. He played football and basketball and ran track in junior high school. It was surprising that he had a nonchalant attitude; yet, he was successful at anything he attempted. I made the track team in junior high and ran the 440-yard dash and mile run. I attempted to run the hurdles and throw the discus but didn't make either of the hurdles or discus squads.

In June 1967, we bid farewell to junior high, and anxiously looked forward to our sophomore year at Claremont High School. A month before school started, boys desiring to try out for the football team reported to the high school practice field.

I didn't play football in junior high. I tried out for the team in eighth grade because Brad and most of my friends made the team, but I was cut after tryouts.

I made it through the first difficult week, but the junior varsity drills were new to me. I was awkward. I couldn't throw the ball well, nor could I catch. The practice field was hard and dry. The scorching sun drained my energy, and I took frequent breaks to regain my breath. We weren't allowed water breaks until a full team break. Each time I took a personal break, a coach yelled for me to get my butt back on the field. I was humiliated when I hit the sled with the coach riding atop and it didn't budge.

I wasn't cut until the second week of practice. Each day the aspiring players entered the locker room and quickly approached the bulletin board where the coaches posted the cut list. Each day I entered the gym from the practice field, allowing most of the team to go first. I walked through the hallway and past the track team locker room and into the football locker room. The room reeked from the smell of sweat, soiled uniforms, and spray deodorants. The banter from my teammates bounced off the walls, and the clanging of locker doors closing and equipment slapping on metal hangers created a zoo-like atmosphere. I entered and walked slowly to the bulletin board and spied the list and let my eyes travel from the As to the Js. There it is was--right after Darryl Irving--Steve Jackson. I was cut.

My heart sank with embarrassment. My face flushed. Several players patted me on the back.

"Too bad, Steve," Tommy Phillips said, slapping my rear.

"Sorry, Jackson," another player whispered.

With my head hung low, I turned and faced Brad. He had already seen the list and waited for me. I appreciated his gesture.

"Don't let it get you down, pal," he said and rubbed my hair. "There are more important things in life than football."

"Yeah, that's easy for you to say," I replied with a smirk and walked to my locker to change and retrieve my extra jock strap, salt tablets, mouthpiece, and toiletry items. I wanted to leave before hearing more sympathetic comments. I skipped the mandatory shower.

The student manager cleared the uniforms, pads, and cleats from the lockers of the boys that were cut. The white piece of tape bearing my name was stripped from above my locker, erasing the last remnant of my having been part of the team. Throughout the locker room hung pictures of former star athletes who played sports at Claremont and continued to play in college. One former football player played for the Cleveland Browns following an outstanding collegiate career at Syracuse. I walked the room and eyed the photos one last time. I recognized a basketball player my sister dated in high school. I questioned how many of my current classmates would grace that esteemed wall one day. I was envious of their accomplishments. It was time to leave.

I had mixed emotions. I was disappointed, yet relieved to be cut. I didn't want to play football. I wasn't a good player; yet, I realized that I had to give it a shot in case there was a miracle and I made the team. That wasn't going to happen because I never played on a competitive team. Filled with regret, I wished I had played in junior high. Anger at my father surfaced because he never taught or encouraged me to play a sport. I was partially to blame because I didn't show initiative until Brad moved next door.

There wasn't any doubt that Brad would make the team. He played tailback. He was fast and possessed good ball skills. Football was a full-time commitment. There was practice every day, team meetings, game nights, weight training, and weekend film reviews. Brad was consumed with football, and I searched for new activities and friends to occupy my time.

Skip McDuffy was a senior. I don't remember when or how we met. We simply became friends. Brad was consumed with athletics and the Kings, a social club he joined, and Skip replaced him as my closest friend until he graduated. He briefly influenced me as much as Brad.

He drove a 1955 Ford coupe. It was a hot car. He dated Sandy Channing for two years and gave his Juniors Social Club pin and senior class ring to her, signifying they were pre-engaged and couldn't date anyone else. She wore the pin on her blouse every day and the ring on a chain around her neck. They were inseparable. Although public displays of affection were not allowed on school grounds, they normally were wrapped in each other's arms and occasionally stole kisses between classes.

Skip and Sandy often invited me on Friday or Saturday nights to cruise McDonald's and other teen spots along Kingston Pike. When I received my driver's license, I returned the favor. I am unsure why McDonald's became the teen hangout. It was the newest restaurant, and cars drove in circles around the establishment. Guys liked to drive around slowly to show off their cars and search for who else was there. The congestion became overwhelming and McDonald's hired a cop to patrol the area on weekends and keep traffic moving. He resembled Barney Fife on *The Andy Griffith Show* and inherited the nickname Barney. He was as goofy as the real Barney. Once a car made two revolutions around McDonald's, he ordered the driver to leave the premises.

Skip and I cruised alone when Sandy was busy with her social club activities or family obligations. He provided my first beer, Pabst Blue Ribbon, which I was unable to finish. It tasted awful, and I was afraid that my parents would smell it on my breath. I chewed an entire pack of Juicy Fruit gum to hide the odor. When I arrived home, I sped to my bedroom, claiming exhaustion in response to my parents calling from the living room, "How was your evening?"

Skip, Sandy, my date, and I doubled to see The Supremes in concert at the Stokely Athletic Center on the University of Tennessee campus in April. They were the hottest Motown group, and we were thrilled to see Diana Ross in person. Following the concert, we had dinner at the Tennessean Restaurant on Cumberland Avenue near campus. Although I was a sophomore, I felt older and more mature, going to a concert and dinner with a date. I was indebted to Skip for hanging out with a sophomore. I found myself acting completely different than I did with Brad.

We became addicted to concerts and added The Four Seasons; Peter, Paul, and Mary; Chicago; Sonny and Cher; and the Joe Tex Show, featuring Percy Sledge, the Delfonics, and the Intruders to our list. The highlight was a trip to Chattanooga for a concert featuring Gary Lewis and the Playboys, the Kinks, and Paul Revere and the Raiders. I was surprised my parents allowed me to travel that far with Skip and Sandy, but since Skip was older, they judged him to be responsible. I couldn't find a date whose parents would allow her to attend a concert in Chattanooga. Skip preferred that Brad not attend, and the three of us made the trip and thoroughly enjoyed the concert.

Mid-way through my sophomore year, Sandy introduced me to Karen Collins. I experienced childhood crushes, but nothing serious. Karen was my first true love. She was a year older and a member of the Star Lites Social Club. She had shoulder length blonde hair and baby blue eyes. She had a radiant smile and loved to joke and give me a hard time. Since she and Sandy were such close friends, we were the perfect foursome. Karen and I talked constantly on the phone, with my parents often yelling at me to get off the phone and do my homework. We spent time talking between classes and ate lunch together every day. Brad accused me of being pussy whipped, and I didn't deny it.

We dated several months, often doubling with Skip and Sandy. Each year Karen's social club had a formal dance at Beaver Creek Country Club, and she invited me to attend that Spring. It was my first formal, and since I was a sophomore, I was fortunate to attend. Only juniors and seniors normally attended.

Luckily, I owned a nice suit, and Skip reminded me to buy a corsage for Karen.

Skip picked up Sandy and me before going to Karen's house. I was nervous even though I'd already met her parents. I was glad that Skip and Sandy went to the door with me. Her father greeted us and invited us inside. He said Karen would be down in a minute. Karen walked into the room, and my eyes glanced at the most beautiful site I'd ever seen. She was stunning, dressed in a gorgeous light blue gown that made her eyes glow. I almost said wow aloud. I stood speechless. Skip bailed me out by reminding me to give the corsage to Karen. I walked over and handed the corsage to her.

"You look beautiful," I said. She smiled and handed the corsage to her mother who pinned it on her dress. Her mother pinned a boutonniere in the buttonhole of my lapel. We posed for the obligatory pictures and listened to her parents' cautions about being careful before we finally escaped.

Skip asked an older friend to buy two half-pints of cherry vodka, and we drank the bottles on the way to the dance. Sandy and Karen did not drink much, and Skip drank most of one bottle. He was drunk, and I pretended to be intoxicated. Guys often pretended to be drunk. It was the cool thing to do.

I survived my first formal. It was the best time I'd had in my brief high school career, and luckily, we weren't caught drinking and didn't have an accident. Skip threw up in the restroom at the country club, and I drove home, although I didn't have a driver's license. I nervously drove the speed limit and took Karen and Sandy home. By the time we reached my house, Skip was sober enough to drive home. He was the talk in the hallways at school on Monday. That was the whole idea anyway, right?

....

With two months left before Summer break, the

weather warmed, the dogwoods and daffodils were blooming, and we suffered from cabin fever. We spent weekends at Watts Bar Lake, partying, swimming, boating, and water skiing. Although the water was cold, after a few beers, several of the gathered group braved the water to swim and ski.

Brad bragged that he could ski without getting wet by starting from the dock. I had no idea that he knew how to water ski. I didn't imagine Iowa as a place to water ski, but little did I know. We dared him, and he readily accepted the challenge. He put on his life vest and sat on the edge of the dock. He put on the water skis and rested them on the water.

"Ready!" he shouted to the boat's driver.

The engine roared as the boat sped forward. The ski rope pulled taut, almost taking Brad's arms out of their sockets. A group of us cheered "go, go, go" from the bank as Brad struggled to keep his balance, swaying side to side, then floated away on the silken surface, shooting his middle finger from a distance. We cheered and laughed. Brad never ceased to amaze us.

Although he succeeded in getting up on the skis without getting wet, it was a different scene when he was ready to quit. He tried to ski into shore but fell short of his goal and sank into the freezing water, while we howled with laughter from the dock.

I had never skied and made several attempts but failed to make it up. My arms grew tired, my eyes blurred from the splashing water, and my mouth flooded with the cold, murky lake water because I refused to let go of the ski rope while the boat drug me. Frustrated and exhausted, I finally let go of the rope. I learned to ski before Summer's end, and it became a favorite sport for me. Those days spent on the lake were filled with laughter and good times. None of us had a care in the world and secretly wished it would last forever.

Skip cornered me in the hallway one Friday and asked if Karen and I wanted to double with him and Sandy to the Skyway Drive-In in Oak Ridge. That drive-in was the closest one to us, and it wasn't a far drive. His car was in the shop, and Karen was driving, which was why he wanted to double because he rarely doubled to the drive-in. I wouldn't have my driver's license for a few months, and Karen asked me to drive once we were a safe distance from my house. She knew that I had driven home from the formal and trusted my driving skills. I had my learner's permit, which was good during daylight hours when accompanied by a licensed driver. Sandy and Skip wanted the back seat.

Many weekend outings were held at the Skyway. The management charged per person in each car when the car stopped at the ticket booth. We occasionally hid one or two guys in the car's trunk to avoid paying, and once settled at a parking space, the stowaways exited the trunk. The theater management became wise to the scheme and stationed staff with walkie talkies in the parking lot, and once the offending patrons exited the trunk, they were approached and charged the entrance fee.

One weekend, I attended with some social club buddies, and when we stopped to pay for two of us who were visible to the ticket seller, two other members in the trunk assumed we arrived at our parking space and exited the trunk at the ticket booth in front of the ticket seller. It was a humiliating moment, and we laughed about it the remainder of the night and far into the next week.

I wish that I remember the name of the movie we saw on our double date. It may have been *Butch Cassidy and the Sundance Kid,* but I simply can't remember. It was a special evening for me, and it's unfortunate that I don't remember what movie was showing when I lost my virginity. Skip's influence played a role in the evening's outcome.

I confess that Karen and I wouldn't have done anything had Skip and Sandy not commenced doing something in the back seat.

The movie was thirty minutes in when Skip and I started making out with our dates. I heard heavy moaning coming from the back seat, and I suspected Karen heard it. I heard Sandy softly whisper, "Please don't get me pregnant." I realized that they were doing *the dirty deed*. I opened one eye to steal a glance to confirm my suspicion. It was the consummate peer pressure. Their love making contributed to our arousal, and one thing led to another. Karen's and my petting became heavier. My hands caressed her body and she massaged my upper thigh. Our kissing became intense, and I briefly opened an eye and discovered the car windows were completely fogged.

My hand slipped under her shirt and made its way to her breasts. Simultaneously, she rubbed my crotch, and I feared a premature ejaculation. We stopped and fumbled to pull down our pants. It was difficult with the steering wheel being an obstacle. Most guys carried a rubber in their wallet, and I was fortunate that I had one in mine. It had been secluded there for over a year, and I prayed it was still good. My pants were at my knees, and I struggled to find my wallet. I removed the rubber and hurriedly opened the package and put it on. Karen recognized I was having trouble, and she helped to guide me in.

I was clumsy. I was premature. I was embarrassed. It wasn't Karen's first time, and she didn't know it was mine, although it was obvious. We never discussed that evening. I didn't tell Brad or anyone. It's ironic. Guys normally bragged about sex when they hadn't had it, and when I finally could tell the truth, I chose to remain silent. It was special, and I wanted to keep it private.

Skip never mentioned that night. He probably assumed that it wasn't my first time because when we discussed sex, I lied about previous encounters. He often kidded me that my favorite past time was jacking off, and he continued to harass me long after Friday night.

9

I can't explain why I decided to join the Royals Social Club. I attribute it to peer pressure.

Claremont High School's social activities were dominated by several underground social clubs, including Karen's Star Lites. There were three men's clubs, the Kings, the Juniors, and the Royals, and like college fraternities, there was a rank order of prestige.

The Kings were what their name implied--the kings of everything at school. The top athletes, the studs, and the rich boys were Kings. The Juniors were their biggest competitor for members, and the Royals, for the most part, weren't chosen by the other two. The Royals were good guys and developed their own unique identity. They had a strong brotherhood, and most of them would not have joined one of the other two clubs even if asked. They liked being Royals.

The clubs had a gentlemen's agreement to not deliver bids on the same night shortly after school commenced in the Fall. This ensured that they wouldn't inadvertently meet at one of the few houses where they might bid on the same person. There was an intense rivalry, and on occasion, fights erupted between rival club members. It was unacceptable to have a fight at the home of a potential member. If that occurred, the prospect might be discouraged from joining either club.

The clubs leaked the dates when bids would be offered to ensure that aspiring members would be home when the caravan of club members arrived. Following a club meeting at the president's house when the final bid list was approved, the members piled into their vehicles and visited each potential pledge's house to extend the offer in person. The clubs had a sweetheart, and she made the journey with the members to seal the bid with a kiss for individuals who accepted the bid.

The third Thursday night in September was the Kings' bid night. I assumed I wasn't going to get a bid, but like winning the lottery, I prayed for a miracle. The Kings chose that day because Claremont's football team played at home the next night, and the non-football player pledges were paraded and made spectacles at the game and dance afterward. Individuals receiving bids were expected to be home when the Kings arrived.

Brad said he wasn't fond of the social clubs. He believed they deprived independence, and he detested being told what to do. He was afraid that he would hit an active member who hazed him. However, he refused to say that he absolutely wouldn't join. I told him that it would be neat if we both got bids from the Kings so that we could go through the experience together.

"I'll face that decision when the time comes," he said, inferring that he was interested in the Kings.

Thursday night arrived and I created activities to remain occupied and pass the time. After supper, I rushed to my room and completed a thorough cleaning. I finished my homework. I wrote a pen pal in Morocco. I played a Dylan album. I watched the clock.

I lay on my bed, staring blankly at the ceiling, realizing Brad was across the street experiencing the same nervous excitement. I wanted to visit and play cards, shoot baskets, or do anything, but I didn't want to be there when the Kings arrived to extend his bid, knowing I probably wouldn't receive one. It would be embarrassing and humiliating. My presence would create an awkward situation for the Kings if they weren't going to bid me, too.

Yet, I prayed that I was on the bid list. It was common knowledge that Brad and I were friends, and perhaps that tipped the vote in my favor. "I hope Brad put in a good word for me.

God, to be a King," I silently pondered. I would do anything, even endure their brutal initiation.

My dreams and prayers were in vain.

The clock read 7:30 when I heard the blaring horns across the street disturbing the evening's quiet. My heart raced, my hands shook, and my ears stayed alert for the knock that never came.

"What the hell is that racket?" I heard Dad yell from the living room.

"I don't know," Mom responded.

Pacing the floor in my room, I refused to admit my disappointment by watching the activity from my window, like the day I watched Brad move in across the street a few years earlier.

I never discussed the social clubs with my parents because they wouldn't approve my membership. They frowned on outside activities and encouraged academics, hoping I would receive a college scholarship. Regardless, I decided to join, if asked, and not inform them until long after initiation, if, in fact, I survived. That's a story for later.

I heard Dad's easy chair creak as he rose to check the commotion. I stayed in my room, attuned to what I couldn't see.

Dad said, "A bunch of kids are at the Ericksons."

"Probably the football team," Mom responded, busying herself with some mindless task.

"No, it's the Kings," I said to myself.

Ten minutes passed, and car horns again blared, and voices chanted as the Kings departed. Brad had kissed Patti Evans, the Kings' sweetheart, had accepted a Kings sweatshirt, and become a Kings pledge. He joined them to disseminate the remainder of the bids and was used as bait to convince other sophomores to accept their bid.

Because Brad expressed that he was unsure if he would

join the Kings, I hoped that he declined. I imagined that he asked if they were going to give his good friend, Steve, a bid, and they responded no, resulting in him telling them to stick the bid up their ass and get the hell out. Once the Kings departed, he would come to my house and detail what he had done, and I would be forever indebted to my best friend. I was dreaming, and I knew it.

I continued my thoughts aloud, "I know. They'll be back later. They're just playing games with me. Brad's a prankster and told them to return later."

I waited. Nine o'clock. Ten o'clock. No horns. No shouting. No Kings. No bid. I went to bed, deeply hurt and disappointed. That night brought distance to our friendship.

The next day was humiliating. I didn't want to go to school but knew my mother wouldn't buy a contrived illness. I was rarely sick and never missed school.

Brad and I met at the bus stop.

"Hey," he called.

"Hey," I responded, refusing to meet his eyes. I was angry.

There was a brief silence. Who would break the ice?

Brad kicked the pavement with his shoe and said, "I guess you heard the Kings last night."

"Yeah." I paused. "You get a bid?"

"Yeah." He hesitated. "I accepted it."

"Congratulations," I said.

"Thanks."

"When's initiation?" I asked with genuine interest.

"Next weekend, I presume."

"Damn, I bet you dread it"

"You ain't shittin'."

My anger increasing, I wanted to hear the details of the previous evening. I was tired of the nice guy exchange. "Who else got in?"

Brad mentioned a dozen names, which I recognized.

"Billy Rivers?" I laughed. "You've got to be kidding. How did that piece of shit get in?"

"His big brother was a King. It's that legacy thing. They had no choice. His brother drove over from UT to help extend the bid to him," Brad replied.

"So Billy Rivers gets a bid, and I don't? Did you put in a good word for me? We do everything together."

Brad paused and stared at me. "What the fuck do I have to do with who they give bids to?"

"You have more influence than you realize. You're big shit on campus. We're friends. All you had to do was let them know I wanted a bid, too."

"I didn't think about it."

"Yeah, sure."

"Look, Steve…."

"Just fucking forget it. What's done is done."

"I'm sorry, maybe in the Spring…"

I interrupted because I didn't want sympathy for not receiving a bid. "Here's our bus," I pointed. I went in first and sat with another student. Brad followed me and sat with someone in the rear of the bus. When we arrived at school, I didn't wait for him. We didn't speak for the remainder of the week.

The word hell doesn't begin to describe the next week for the Kings pledges. Since the Kings were the best club, they were known to have the roughest hell week and initiation. Brad had no idea how difficult that week would be, and I had no sympathy for him.

Brad had to be careful about pledging because the coaches banned athletes from joining the clubs, which made them even more enticing. The club members were cautious when hazing pledges at school to avoid getting caught by administrators, teachers, or coaches. Secret assignments were given, and the pledges were harassed at lunch and in the restrooms.

Pledges avoided going to the restroom in fear of meeting an active member. Many of the worst things happened in the restroom where a pledge was made to do pushups, drink Tabasco sauce, or perform a taffy pull. A taffy pull consisted of grabbing a piece of feces in the toilet and pulling it apart. Why would anyone do that? I learned that there were few things a guy wouldn't do to get initiated into a social club.

Before classes, at lunch, and during breaks, students sat in the hallways and talked. I was sitting outside my algebra class with a group of friends when Brad approached Becky Clifford, a cheerleader, who was sitting with us. He carried a pencil with a string attached. I noticed several Kings standing nearby.

"Hi, Becky," he said, his face turning bright red. "Would you sign my autograph book?"

"Sure," she giggled and grabbed the pencil with a jerk and pulled it toward her. I saw Brad wince in pain, and the students around me laughed. I realized that the other end of the string was tied to his penis.

Becky signed the book, gave the pencil another hard tug, and returned it to Brad. He refused to make eye contact, and with a quick "thank you," turned to rejoin the Kings, who were laughing loudly.

I saw little of Brad that week because he was involved in hell week activities and football practice after school. I didn't want to appear overly interested in his pledging antics, most of which he wouldn't admit. The pledges were sworn to secrecy. I refused to call him because I was still upset about not getting a Kings bid, although I wasn't as angry as I was at the bus stop. He made it through the week basically unscathed. His initiation was Friday night after the Claremont and Halls football game.

All three clubs' pledges sat in the same vicinity at the game. There were few pranks and harassment since it was public. The pledges were sent to the concession stand for food and drinks for the actives and performed group cheers, standing arm-in-arm. One club's pledge joined a line dance with the cheerleaders, but he was drunk and enjoyed it more than he was humiliated. I was surprised that pledges were allowed to drink.

Following the game, we attended a dance at the National Guard Armory, where the club pledges were abused. The football player pledges arrived late because they held a team meeting and showered before attending the dance. Once he arrived, Brad was required to dance with an unattractive and obese girl. The Kings failed to realize that few things bothered Brad. His self-confidence was stronger than theirs, and it was difficult to embarrass him. He also slow danced with a pledge brother, which seemed to embarrass him more than dancing with the obese girl.

The Kings left early, parading the pledges through the crowd in a duck walk. I dropped my resentment and shot Brad a thumbs up salute and mouthed the words "good luck" as he departed for initiation. He smiled and said, "Thanks."

Mr. Erickson constantly worked on his house or in the yard. The house needed major repairs and renovation, and he added vast improvements to its appearance. The outside was painted, and he added a nice wooden deck at the rear, where there was no neighboring house. Thick woods covered the back, and the deck was used for lounging in cooler weather and sunbathing in Summer.

His newest project was to clear an area in his back yard to plant a garden. He hired Brad and me to help clear the land of weeds, stumps, and large rocks. Mom woke me early Saturday morning after the night at the Armory dance and Brad's initiation. I told her to go away.

"Steve, you're supposed to help Mr. Erickson today. Time to get up," she said, shaking my shoulder. I stayed late at the dance and didn't get home until 1:30 a.m. I preferred to stay in bed, but I wanted to meet Brad and hear about his initiation. Evidently there was no tragedy, and Brad survived because we didn't receive an early morning phone call.

After gobbling a bowl of corn flakes and ignoring Mom's warning to slow down and remember to brush my teeth, I raced to Brad's house. I spotted him already hard at work, chopping a stubborn tree stump. I immediately saw the damage.

Brad's hair looked like someone attempted to scalp him.

"What the hell happened?" I whispered.

He hushed me because his father was approaching.

"Mornin', Steve," Mr. Erickson said and shook my hand.

"Good morning, sir," I replied. "What would you like me to do?" I found it difficult to avoid staring at Brad's hair.

"I need you and Injun Joe here to work at this old stump," he said, sending Brad a look of disapproval. Brad continued chopping, not acknowledging the comment and stare. "When you get enough of it exposed, I'll try to pull it out with the truck."

"Yes, sir," I shot back, grabbing an ax from the ground.

Mr. Erickson returned to throwing rocks into a wheelbarrow, and I again asked Brad what happened.

"Nothing," he said.

"Nothing my ass. Look at your hair!"

"They put Nair in it." I recognized the name of the infamous hair remover.

"You're shittin' me?" I grinned but dared not laugh. Brad was not amused. He was angry.

I should have changed the subject but remained curious about his initiation. "Man, the coaches will have your balls when they see you on Monday."

"I know. I'm going to get a burr cut this afternoon. I plan to tell the other players who were initiated with me to shave their heads, too, so the coaches will believe the sophomore players got the same haircut as a unity thing." He paused and added, "Maybe we'll start a new tradition." He offered a slight laugh and glanced at me for the first time.

"That's not the only place they put the Nair," he admitted.

"What do you mean?" I asked.

He looked at me with upturned eyes. "Think about it," he said.

I stopped chopping and grabbed my crotch. "You're kidding?"

"Nope. Nair and liquid Heet." Heet was a liniment treatment for sore muscles and other aches and pains. It burns like hell.

My balls ached in sympathy.

"I'm dying right now," he continued. "The sweat is killing me. I showered when I got home and again this morning, but it won't stop burning."

"What did you tell your parents?"

"The truth," he replied. "I don't care. I have nothing to hide."

"I bet they're pissed."

"Pissed doesn't begin to describe it. They're pissed I didn't get home until after 3 this morning. Luckily, they didn't get up when I got home because if they saw what I looked like, they may have called the police."

Brad continued strong swings with the ax and added softly, "Particularly my dad. He said it was stupid and can't believe I did it. They don't know the half of it. He can't believe I jeopardized football for a damn social club. I can't either now that it's over. Be glad you weren't there."

I wasn't sure I liked the last comment. "Hindsight isn't worth shit," I added. "What else did they do to you?"

"I don't want to talk about it anymore. We're not supposed to tell non-members," he said, and realized his slight. "Sorry."

I was hurt but didn't press for further information. We worked the rest of the day with little conversation, Brad's pain subsiding as the day progressed, although he appeared physically exhausted. His idea to convince the other football players initiated with him to shave their heads worked, and the coaches never questioned their motive. They expressed satisfaction that the young men showed a symbol of unity.

Brad passed a major juvenile rite of passage and was further instilled as a teenage icon at Claremont High. I never abandoned my desire to become a King or a Junior, but my wish was in vain.

When I finally heard the car horns and the obnoxious shouting at my house when school resumed in early January, it was the Royals that came calling. I can only guess why I was invited to join the Royals. Dating Karen helped. Being friends with Brad and Skip was an asset. Most of my friends were social club members.

None of the Royals were my close friends. Since Brad was my best friend, I associated with the Kings, but many of my friends, including Skip, were Juniors. I assumed Skip would vouch for me and have them extend a bid, but that never occurred. He and Sandy were so serious that he dropped his active status with the Juniors, unaware that I wanted to join the club. It was something I never had the courage to tell him.

10

Fall 1967 breezed to a close. A local television station sponsored a weekly show called "Discoteen." Students from area schools were invited to join the show and dance to the latest hits. Claremont students were asked to appear in a show to be taped the first weekend in December. Student Council made an announcement that it was first come, first served for 30 students. Brad asked a girl he knew to be his date for the show, and I invited Karen. We made the cut list.

It was an exciting and interesting experience and my first time on television. We were instructed to ignore the cameras, which was not easy. It was hot under the studio lights, and I perspired profusely. The show was broadcast two weeks later, and we gathered at a friend's house to watch, constantly looking for ourselves and laughing at each other.

The next week I awoke to the news that one of my favorite singers, Otis Redding, had died in a plane crash. His best song, (*Sittin' on*) *The Dock of the Bay*, didn't hit number one until after his death. I was sad and wished that I had one of his records to play.

Monday, January 8, 1968. I finished dinner and homework and was lying on my bed, listening to a new Zombies album I'd purchased at Miller's Department Store. I heard car horns and assumed it was a group of Kings or a girl's club members visiting Brad. There was a tradition among club members to blow their car horn whenever they passed the house of a member of their club, or for the girls, a member of a boys' club. Each club developed its own unique horn repetition so that individuals recognized the specific club of the member that had passed. I heard loud knocking on our door and questioned the source.

"Steve, you have visitors," Mom called loudly.

I raced to the front door and was confronted by the Royals' president, Barry Gibson, and the club sweetheart, Julie Graham. I was nervous and bewildered.

"Hey, Steve," Barry said.

"Hey," I responded. Mom remained within hearing distance, and I preferred to go outside. I didn't dare invite the large group inside.

"Can you come outside?" Barry asked, offering rescue.

"Sure," I responded with relief.

I stepped onto the porch and spotted a large group of Royals lining the sidewalk and yard. I naively admit that I was unsure why they were there.

"Steve, how would you like to become a member of the best social club at Claremont High?" Barry boasted.

"The Kings?" I thought to myself with a sly smile before replying, "What do you mean?"

"The Royals met tonight, and they voted unanimously to offer you a bid," he replied. The other members responded with applause and cheers.

With the brief informal ceremony concluded, the Royals erupted in applause and the club chant. I blushed from the attention.

I stole a glace toward Brad's house. I prayed he wasn't home and if so, he wasn't watching. I don't know why it bothered me. I wanted in a club, and the opportunity finally arrived. Barry was speaking again. "What do you say, Steve? Ron Johnson accepted his bid, and we have eight more to give out. It will be a boss pledge class," he said, slapping Ron on the back, who shyly dropped his head. I knew Ron and realized he was a good catch for the Royals. He had played football at the Boys' Club and was popular. I didn't know if he received a bid from the Kings or Juniors, but if he did, he declined because he wasn't in the pledge classes that were initiated in the Fall. If his friends were part of the pact, it certainly would be a good pledge class.

I hesitated and didn't know why. Yes, I did know why. I knew that if I accepted the bid, it would end hope of getting a bid from the Kings or Juniors. Although a member could quit one club and join another if offered an invitation, it rarely happened because few were willing to endure another hell week and initiation.

"Yeah, I accept!" I blurted with a huge smile.

"Great," Barry replied, slapping me on the back and shaking my hand.

Julie stepped up and kissed me on the lips. I blushed as the Royals cheered and applauded. More handshakes and congratulations followed.

"Can you come with us to give out the other bids?" Barry asked. "It'd be great. You know the other guys. It'll be cool for them to know you and Ron are joining."

"Sure. Let me tell my folks," I said, opening the door, thinking quickly what to say to my parents.

"Mom, I'm going over to the Pike with the guys for a while," I called rather than asking permission.

"You've got school tomorrow. Be home in an hour," she replied. I realized that later she would question why the large group of kids visited, and I needed to prepare a false response.

I joined Ron in Barry's car to deliver the remaining bids. Seven of the eight were accepted, and three were Ron's friends. I automatically gained a new peer group with which to bond, and we were united with mutual fear and tense excitement of the unexpected ritual that awaited us.

I knew that I had to tell Brad and decided to call him when I returned home and get it over with. The conversation went well, and he congratulated me. I didn't want to discuss it at length, so I told him I had to go and finish my homework before going to bed.

The next week was hell. We were humiliated at every opportunity and made to perform duties before and after school, during lunch, and between classes. We carried actives' trays at lunch and their books to their classes. We were forced to eat various concoctions made from leftover food at lunch. The cafeteria served small pats of butter and peanut butter, and the actives enjoyed making us cram stacks of them into our mouths and eating the sticky mess. They put hot sauce on our lips with a toothpick every day at lunch.

Ron and I were forced to hold hands and skip down the hall. I was told to kiss him on the cheek and tell him I loved him. I gave him a quick smack on the cheek and pretended to whisper the required message. I pushed a penny with my nose along a sidewalk, and push-ups were a constant requirement. I was forced to put my socks on my hands and sit in the hallway prior to class. I was surprised that we performed so many requirements visibly at school because if an administrator or teacher caught us, the club would be in trouble, and the individuals involved would be disciplined.

The week passed slowly, and the day before initiation, I sat in the hallway with several Juniors and Kings before class commenced when I heard, "Hey, Jackson, dip shit, get over here."

I glanced with humiliation and recognized Paul Alvarez, a Royals active staring harshly at me. I answered his command and felt my friends' eyes following me. Their chatter ceased and they listened to the confrontation.

"What the fuck do you think you're doing, traitor?" Paul said, stabbing my chest with his finger.

Since we were constantly berated for unknown

reasons, my response was sincere. "I don't know what you mean."

"You're sitting with the enemy, you piece of dog shit. I should make you give me twenty-five right here."

"Sorry, Mr. Alvarez. I didn't know it was against the rules," I replied with guarded sarcasm. We were required to address the actives as Mr.

"I'm positive the other Royals won't appreciate your lack of loyalty," he said, swiping his forefinger across my chin. I stole a glance at my friends witnessing the confrontation. There was little sympathy for my situation because they endured similar encounters during their hell weeks. They were curious how it would end. "Should I tell them that you don't want to join the club?"

"No, please don't. Can you let me off this time? I swear I didn't know it was against the rules," I pleaded, regretting my cardinal offense.

He hesitated and said, "Tell, you what, ass wipe. Wash my car after school, and I'll see if I can have a loss of memory."

"Sure," I said with false excitement. "I'm glad to do it."

"Be at my car in the South lot at 3:30, and don't be late," he said, poking his finger in my chest before leaving.

"Yes, sir." I sarcastically saluted as he walked away.

I couldn't believe the mess I created for myself. How stupid I was to sit with the "enemy". I realized that I fell into a trap by accepting to meet him after school because there was an unwritten rule between the pledges to never be alone with an active. There was a rumor that during a hell week in the past, several actives kidnapped a pledge and left him in his underwear stranded in the eastern part of the county near Asheville Highway. The pledge was supposed to return home by any means but was picked up by the cops and taken to the police station where his parents were called to retrieve him. The pledges in my group agreed to tape a dime to the bottom of our foot in case we were kidnapped and abandoned so we could call a pledge brother for help. I'd forgotten to tape a dime to my foot that morning but would do it before meeting Alvarez that afternoon.

I raced to locate Ron before class and provided details about the incident.

"How could you be so fucking stupid?" he lectured.

"I don't know. It just happened," my anger and discomfort evident. "How was I supposed to know that I can't sit in the hallway with my friends? The Royals aren't my only friends."

"Well, don't worry about it. Alvarez is an ass. We'll figure something out. One for all, all for one," he recited our pledge class motto.

"Easy for you to say," I offered as we headed separate ways. "It's not your ass that's on the line."

"You forget that we're all in this together, brother," Ron called from a distance.

I remained in a haze during class the remainder of the day. Fear and anxiety engulfed me, and I was fortunate that I did not have a test because I would have failed.

After the final bell sounded at 3:15, I raced to my locker to retrieve my jacket and books I needed for homework. I ran to the South parking lot, fearing I would miss the ordered arrival time and fall into further trouble.

I spotted several guys milling around Alvarez's car and realized, much to my chagrin, I would be forced to confront additional Royals, but as I edged closer, I recognized Ron and my other pledge brothers, and I heaved a huge sigh of relief. My fear of being kidnapped disappeared.

"What are you guys doing here?" I purposely asked the dumb question.

"One for all, all for one," Ron said with a laugh. The others nodded agreement. "You didn't believe we'd leave you out on a limb by yourself, did you?"

"Thanks, guys," I responded.

"What's this crap?" Alvarez shouted as he approached his car, breaking our camaraderie. "The rest of you shit-for-brains get lost. This matter is between Jackson and me."

"One for all, all for one," Ron repeated. A few "yeahs" sounded from the pledges as we closed ranks.

"I'm warning you. This is your last chance to beat it unless you want to take on the entire club." Alvarez attempted the stern warning, realizing he faced a stand-off and couldn't back down to the pledge class.

"Sorry, no can do," Ron said with persistence. He became our self-proclaimed leader. I was proud he was fighting the battle for me.

There was a tense hesitation in which neither side budged. Alvarez clinched his fists, and his jaw tightened. He was outnumbered, and he had to save face. His face turned red as he struggled for words.

"What's it going to be, clean car or dirty car?" Ron broke the silence.

Alvarez relaxed but refused to admit defeat. He screamed, "All right, you fucking jerkoffs. I have to go to work, but I ain't forgettin' this. Just wait until initiation. You'll pay. Now get the hell out of here."

Ron should have remained quiet but couldn't resist saying, "What about your car wash?"

Alvarez glared at Ron and responded, "I said get the hell out of here, you little piece of shit."

The confrontation ended, and Alvarez glanced angrily toward each pledge. The situation could have ended much worse, and we were visibly relieved to escape the parking lot.

As we turned to leave, Alvarez grabbed Ron by his coat collar, stuck his face into Ron's, and said, "Particularly you, Johnson, I'll remember you. Your ass is grass. You're mine."

We cheered and yelled expletives out of hearing range as Alvarez spun his wheels, spewing dirt and gravel on other cars as he sped away. "Man, his breath stinks," Ron laughed, and we joined him.

We won the battle, but silently accepted the fact that we still had to face the war, one we were guaranteed to lose. There was no doubt that Alvarez intended to kidnap and leave me stranded somewhere. My pledge brothers saved my ass.

It was the longest week of my life and ended as badly as it began. We were subjected to merciless ridicule. The hazing was harsh and humiliating, and I questioned if it was the hazing that bothered me or the fact that I was pledging the Royals. Alvarez didn't inform the Royals about the encounter with the pledges. He would never admit that he relented, assuming he would be labeled a wimp. We joked and bragged about the incident among ourselves, admitting we would pay the price later. We successfully finished the week without another pledge getting caught alone with an active.

Friday arrived. Club initiations were held on Friday or Saturday night following hell week. We were minors, and the actives acknowledged that initiation could not be a surprise because we had to provide excuses to our parents about our whereabouts for the evening. Several pledges lied to their parents about where they were spending the night. I seriously doubt that any parent would have allowed their son to endure a club initiation if they knew what occurred.

Ron became my protector following the incident with Alvarez, and I asked my parents if I could spend Friday night at his house. They offered opposition since they hadn't met him. I promised to have him stop by, which he did, and he met their approval with flying colors.

I truly feared for my life at initiation. Although no one had died, there was a first time for everything. Horror stories about club initiations prevailed, resulting in the administrator and coaches ban on club membership. Pledges suffered injuries, and I prepared for the worst experience of my life. I can't believe I knowingly agreed to undergo something presumed to be extremely dangerous. I also remembered what Brad had experienced. Yet, it became important to me. It was a rite of passage, and I was determined to pass the test.

To further demonstrate my fear, I wrote a note to my parents and hid it in the desk drawer in my room. If I were killed or seriously injured, they would eventually peruse my personal property and locate the note. I wrote that I loved them and asked them to not grieve too much for me. I didn't attempt to explain what I was doing or why, probably because *I* didn't know why.

The actives passed the word to the pledges during school on Friday that we were to meet at McDonald's on the Pike at 10:00 that night. We agreed to meet at Ron's house at 8:00 to share our fears, discuss a plan for the approaching nightmare, and bond as brothers facing a common, unknown fate.

One pledge, Scott Schultz, failed to arrive at the assigned meeting time, creating a problem because we were supposed to be a unified group, each pledge forming a link in a chain. If one link broke or was missing, the chain became useless. We feared that if Scott failed to show, initiation would be postponed, and we had experienced too much not to be initiated. We unanimously agreed we would not endure another hell week. We weren't aware that the actives would initiate us without the missing pledge because they needed us to increase their numbers for various activities and the money provided through our membership dues.

We spent an hour planning strategy and agreed to stick together at initiation and not allow anyone to be taken away alone. We concluded that if the situation got out of control and it appeared someone might get hurt, we would abandon initiation as a group. We determined there was power in numbers and that the entire pledge class would not be dismissed from the club. They needed us because several actives were graduating that Spring.

Our worry increased with the passage of time. We continually called Scott's house, but there was no answer.

"What the hell are we going to do?" a pledge asked.

"We have to leave soon if we're going to make it by 10:00," another offered.

"Just chill, guys," Ron assured. "He'll make it. I know it. He's always late."

No sooner than Ron spoke than the doorbell rang. We were in the basement, and Ron sprang to his feet and sprinted up the stairs, conquering three steps at a time. He reappeared with Scott, slowly following him.

"Where were you?" we asked with unified relief and anger. Someone threw a basketball at him.

"Hey, don't worry about it, guys. Chill. He's here. That's the important thing. We need to hit the road," Ron instructed. We recited our pledge class motto, pushed each other jokingly, and departed to confront what waited ahead.

We arrived at McDonald's, and several Royals leaned on their cars, waiting our arrival. They had been drinking and getting mentally prepared for initiation. We arrived in two cars and parked at Cas Walker's Supermarket across the street to avoid Barney the cop having our cars towed at McDonald's while we were away. We weren't allowed to drive to initiation.

Paul Alvarez was the first to spot us. "Hey, douche bags," he barked. "Get your asses over here!"

"On the double, girls!" cried another active.

"And the shit begins," I sighed. With mutual back pats and wishes for good luck, we crossed the street to commence the long-dreaded ordeal. We arrived, and Alvarez immediately ordered us to do twenty-five push-ups, which drew the attention of McDonald's customers. I wondered why Barney wasn't breaking up the activity.

Many of the actives journeyed ahead to the initiation site, a location which wasn't disclosed to us. The ones left to greet us loaded the nine of us in the back of a pick-up truck and headed West on Kingston Pike, followed by two horn-honking cars of screaming, intoxicated actives.

Once we were clear of witnesses, the truck pulled to the side of the road, and we were blindfolded and told to lie down in the truck's bed. The conditions were cramped, but none dared challenge the orders.

I learned later that our initiation was held on private property owned by the United States Atomic Energy Commission in Anderson County, near Oak Ridge. It was risky, but the actives believed the chances of getting caught late at night were slim. They followed a lengthy dirt road, the roughness bouncing our bodies in the back of the truck. We finally came to a stop, and the actives dragged us from the truck and removed our blindfolds.

The January weather was cold, and we shivered from both the night air and fear. A visible dew, which sparkled through the glowing full moon, covered the ground. I spotted a body of water, which I assumed was the Clinch River. I've often wondered what we were exposed to at that site. There were rumors about secret experiments on animals, and we considered ourselves lucky we were not greeted by two-headed mutants.

"You assholes keep your mouths shut and don't speak

unless you're told to," an active bellowed, and added, "Remember to say yes, sir, and no, sir."

"Yes, sir," a few pledges responded.

"Who gave you dip shits permission to speak?" the active screamed.

There was silence.

"On your stomachs and give me twenty for disobeying orders."

We dropped to the ground and completed the task. While we exercised, actives sat or stood on our backs, making the push-ups more difficult. If we failed to lift from the ground, additional push-ups were added.

"On your feet, piss ants," a voice sounded from the darkness.

We responded, dirt and debris falling from our clothing. "Get in a straight line and face me," the order continued.

We stared ahead, afraid to make eye contact, much less move. I breathed heavily from the exercising and saw my breath in the cool air, which stank of stale beer and urine.

"Bend over and grab your ankles, girls," the active demanded, "and don't let go or you'll regret it."

We followed the directive. The next sound echoing in the night was a large splat, which sounded like a plank landing on concrete. I heard a painful scream and saw one of my pledge brothers fall face forward to the ground. I saw an active brandishing a paddle. There was resounding laughter and loud cheers.

"On your feet, douche bag. You were told not to move. Can't you follow simple orders, dick face?" the active shouted as the pledge struggled to his feet and assumed the position.

"Please, sir, may I have another? Let me hear you say it!" the active ordered the pledge.

The neophyte responded as instructed, but was met with the cry, "Louder!" He repeated the response and endured another strike.

Up and down the line the paddles slammed our butts. The first hits were extremely painful, but eventually, my skin deadened to the pain and I felt only the thrust of the blow. I heard the whimpers of some of my pledge brothers once the pain became unbearable, but I refused to let them get to me, at least not yet. Ron stood adjacent to me, and I realized he was being hit several times without stopping. I stole a glance and recognized the abuser was Alvarez. "Son-of-a-bitch," I said to myself.

The actives spewed endless insults and other demeaning activities at us for an hour. I prayed for an end to the brutality. We ran relay races, exercised, and danced the cancan while singing the Claremont fight song. We recited the *Pledge of Allegiance*.

"All right, ladies, down with your pants and underwear and drop to your knees," a command sounded, and most of us complied.

For the first time, there was hesitation, but a few neophytes quickly unfastened their belts, and the sound of zippers was heard amid the heavy breathing of exhausted pledges. The full moon provided bright light for the activity. A cool breeze flowed through the trees and off the water, and my body continued to shake from the cold and fear.

"Do as I say unless you want the paddle again," the active warned.

We pulled down our pants and underwear and fell to our knees on the ground.

"All right, girls, we're going to have a little elephant walk. Stick your left thumb in your mouth and your right thumb in the ass of the baby elephant in front of you," the directive was given with laughter.

There was no hesitation, at least on my part and the pledge behind me. I closed my fist and pretended to stick my thumb in the rear of the pledge in front of me. The pledge behind me did the same.

"Elephants, switch thumbs!" the new order came and was repeated faster and faster. I heard rowdy laughing and chanting, "Go, go, go! Switch! Switch! Switch!" The atmosphere resembled a frenzied mob scene. I was frightened and would have done anything I was told.

"On your stomachs," an active yelled

"Faces in the dirt," another chimed.

I heard talking, but nothing happened, and my fright increased. I felt it. The warm liquid warmed my body, chilled by the night air. The odor reached my nose, and my stomach turned. I fought the urge to vomit when I discovered that they were urinating on us.

I felt another liquid flowing over my head and body but didn't recognize it. The smell reached my nose, and I saw the thick, gravy-like liquid roll over my crossed arms and soak the ground. They poured motor oil on us, followed by flour.

"Turn over," came the command. We followed directions, our pants and underwear still pulled to our knees. One of the actives walked slowly down the line pouring a liquid on our genitals. The smell of liquid Heet arrived at the same time our balls began burning with unbearable pain. The pain was intense, and I prayed the abuse would end soon. Moans sounded from the defeated pledges. I remembered that Brad had the same experience at his initiation.

"Okay, faggots, pull up your pants and tidy whities and take a swim," the command sounded.

We didn't move because we were puzzled by the command. "Get your asses in the water!" the voice cried.

We scurried to our feet, pulling up our underwear and pants, and walked to the water's edge. I hated everything that we endured, but nothing seemed life-threatening until the order to jump into the water. I knew it was dangerous for us to go into the water. It was dark, and we didn't know how deep it was. I hoped everyone could swim. As we walked slowly and cautiously into the freezing cold water, we heard the actives cheering and yelling, and we turned toward the commotion. The actives were fleeing toward their vehicles.

"Welcome to the Royals, pussies," a shout sounded from the distance.

"What's going on?" I asked Ron. "Where are they going?"

"They're leaving. It's over," he replied.

It *was* over. We survived the melee. We were Royals. Could anyone truly analyze what had happened and why we had voluntarily endured the ordeal?

We returned to the shore, and Ron asked, "Is everyone okay?"

Everyone nodded, mostly unseen in the darkness. A few "yeahs" were heard.

"My ass is killing me," one initiate said.

"I'm freezing," another added, his teeth chattering.

"My balls are burning off," came an additional cry. "I can't stand it."

"Let's get the hell out of here in case they come back," Ron said, and several of the new initiates voiced agreement.

I was amazed by the comments expressed by my peers while we slowly trudged the dirt road. The conversations varied from how bad initiation was to how it wasn't as bad as expected. I glanced toward Ron and was overcome with shock. "What the hell happened to your hair?" I asked.

"Oh, Jesus, I forgot about that. Someone cut it when I

was on the ground," he said, rubbing his hand through the chopped coiffure. "I believe it was that son-of-a-bitch, Alvarez," he added.

"I bet it was," I said. "He said he'd get even with you. I saw him paddling you several times. He's such an asshole."

Too tired to express concern, Ron asked, "How does my hair look?"

"Pretty bad," someone said.

I spotted lights flash briefly from a side road.

"What was that?" I asked.

"I don't know. I hope it's not the AEC patrol," came a reply.

"Maybe it's the Royals hiding and ready to continue the crap," someone added.

"It's over, man," Ron said. "We're not going through anymore shit. I dare them to try something. We're Royals."

"Maybe we should beat it," another offered.

"Jackson," my name was called from the darkness. "Over here."

I paused with confusion and exchanged glances with Ron. "Who is it?" I asked, visions of Alvarez dancing in my head.

"Get your ass over here!" the voice replied in a hoarse shout.

Ron and I led the group cautiously toward the voice and the unknown vehicle. A figure approached, and as it neared, I recognized Brad.

"What the hell are you doing here?" I asked, and added, "The Royals will kill you if they find you here."

"I know," he said. "Come on, hurry up, and get in the back of the truck so we can get the hell out of here. I'll give you a ride back."

I knew how risky it was for him to crash a rival club's

initiation, particularly if he saw or heard anything forbidden to outsiders. "God, I can't believe you followed us," I told him.

"Hey, I couldn't let my buddy down, could I?" he chuckled and slapped me on the back. "Uh, what's this shit?" he asked, wiping his oil-stained hand on his jeans.

"Motor oil," I replied. "Whose truck is this?"

"Benny Smith's," he said.

"Let's go guys, get in the back," I said to the new Royals, "and not a word of this to anyone. We don't have to tell them how we got back. We're Royals now, and they can't do anything more to us. It's our secret. Okay?" My peers nodded agreement, thankful for the rescue. The one thing we forgot to discuss at Ron's house was how we would get home following initiation. I presumed that one of the Royals would take us back to our cars. Brad came to our rescue.

Brad dropped us near our cars. "You okay?" he asked me.

"I'm fine, really," I assured him. "I'm alive, and that's all that matters. Thanks, Brad, we really appreciate it."

"Don't mention it," he laughed, and added, "Don't worry, I'll collect!"

"I know," I said. "That's what I'm afraid of."

"You don't look half as bad as I did after my initiation," he laughed.

"My ass hurts like hell, and my balls are burning off," I said, knowing Brad could sympathize with my agony.

"Don't remind me," he responded.

"How long were you there?" I asked. "Did you see any of it?"

"I followed once they left McDonald's. I was afraid they saw me when they stopped and blindfolded you. Once they turned onto the private property, I turned off my lights and followed their taillights. Luckily, they didn't hear me. I saw them slowing and I pulled off to that side road where you saw me. I walked to where they took you, but I kept my distance in case I was spotted. No telling what they would have done to me had I been caught. I heard all the crap going on but couldn't see much. It seemed to go on forever, and I felt for you. I really did."

"Worst thing I've experienced in my life," I replied. "Now I know why you were in such pain from the Heet. My balls will never recover."

"At least you were spared the Nair."

"I'm glad, but that fucker Alvarez cut Ron's hair. We'll get even with him. Just wait and see. We'll find a way."

"It's over, bro. Put it behind you. He'll act like your best friend. You're brothers now."

I didn't respond. I was exhausted and wanted to leave. Ron was waiting impatiently for me to finish my conversation. "Thanks again, Brad. As you always say to me, I owe you big time!"

"Don't worry about it," he said, honking the horn as he drove from the parking lot.

We walked to Ron's car, hoping to be unseen, particularly by any Royals who might seize the opportunity to further our humiliation. We took cardboard boxes from the trash dumpster at Cas Walker's to cover the car seat so our clothes wouldn't soil them. We congratulated the remaining pledge brothers one last time for surviving the nightmare and headed to Ron's house.

Ron's parents hadn't arrived home from an evening engagement, and we didn't have to sneak into his house. Brad learned from his initiation and warned me to wear clothes that I could throw away. Fortunately, I followed his advice. There was a shower in the Johnson's basement, so after discarding our soiled clothes in a paper bag, we showered and washed away the dirt, urine, and motor oil. Remembering my discussion with Brad, I was thankful I escaped the Nair and the dreadful haircut.

"I can't believe they pissed on us. So fucking gross," I called from the shower and scrubbed the oil from my head.

My butt, blackened from the beatings, ached as the water pelted the tender skin.

"Your hair's a mess," I laughed at Ron. "Your folks will be pissed."

"I know," he replied. "I'll have to shave my head. I'll let you do it before they get home."

"Do you trust me?"

"I don't have much choice, do I? Just remember, payback is hell if you fuck up!"

"You'll still have to have an excuse as to why you shaved your head."

"I'll come up with something. I'll tell them a bunch of us decided to do it to be cool. Shave yours, too, so they'll believe me."

"No way, José. I like you, but not that much."

"Oh, well. It was worth asking."

The next week at school, I proudly wore my Royals active pin. Administration didn't mind that club members wore their pins because they were nice jewelry. We weren't allowed to wear club jerseys at school, but I wore mine at every opportunity for the remainder of the school year. The pride I lacked prior to initiation was earned, although beaten into me, that memorable Friday night. The stories we shared about initiation grew worse and more exaggerated each time they were exchanged. I informed my parents that I joined a club at school called the Royals but never mentioned initiation. Fortunately, I remembered to discard the secret note I left in my desk drawer.

I never wanted to be a Royal but wanted to be in a club.

My friends remained the same, and I didn't have intimate Royals friends, not even among my pledge brothers. Ron and I were never as close again as the night we shared initiation, showered, and talked into the wee hours of the morning about the shared hell we experienced. We eventually went our separate ways.

I participated in Royals activities and maintained an interest in the club. In the Fall, we earned money cleaning the football stadium on Saturday mornings following a home game the previous night. The Kings and Juniors competed in an annual football game which drew large numbers from the other clubs. I convinced Brad to use his influence with the Kings to play a game against the Royals. I was proud that we attracted a large crowd. I prayed for a Royals victory, but we lost 27-7. I was convinced that the more visible the Royals became by participating in positive activities, our reputation would improve; thus, attracting a better quality of members in the future.

A year later, I was elected Royals president but resigned and quit the club the Fall of my senior year when I failed to convince the membership to eliminate hazing from initiation. I was friends with several of the new sophomores, mostly athletes, and believed I could convince them to join if they were guaranteed that hazing was abolished. I presented a proposal at a Royals meeting, but it was met with negative sarcasm. "That makes us pussies," one active said.

Another added, "They need to earn membership like we did." I attempted to convince them that if we treated the pledges with dignity, they would respect us more. It fell on deaf ears, and the opposition increased. I lingered long over my decision to resign, concluding that I no longer wanted to be part of a group which participated in a barbaric initiation rite.

The week following my decision, I went shopping with

my mother, and while there, a group of Royals visited my house. They hoped to convince me to change my mind and remain in the club. I was fortunate to be away because I probably would have given in to the peer pressure and returned to the club.

There was one moment of insanity my junior year when I considered quitting the Royals and joining the Juniors and enduring the tribulation again. I mentioned to a Juniors friend that I would seriously consider quitting the Royals and joining the Juniors if I received a bid. No bid was extended, and I was spared the agonizing decision. Was I crazy?

11

Five years after President Kennedy's death, two more killings joined the list of events in my life I'll never forget. April 4, 1968 became another day among many I vividly recall. I was studying in my room that Thursday night when my parents summoned me to the living room to watch a news bulletin on television announcing that Dr. Martin Luther King, Jr. had been assassinated 400 miles away in Memphis.

"My God, I can't believe it!" my mother exclaimed, her hand covering her mouth.

"This is scary," my father added, dropping his newspaper, and shaking his head.

I worried about the reaction following the assassination. Racial tensions were heightened throughout the country, particularly the South. Memphis was far from Knoxville, but since it was in the same state, I feared local repercussions.

"The whole damn country will riot," Dad said.

Overcome with anxiety about the potential results of the felled civil rights leader, I asked, "What should we do?" I had visions of civil war and innocent people dying.

"We're definitely staying put until we learn more," Dad replied adamantly.

"Maybe they'll cancel school tomorrow," I said, a bit too eager, considering the occasion.

"Even if they don't, you're not leaving this house," Mom said, placing an assuring hand on my shoulder.

We were glued to the news and heard reactions from various leaders, including President Johnson, who compared the shooting to that of his predecessor, and canceled a trip to Hawaii for a weekend conference on the war in Vietnam.

Dad's prediction that rioting would break out across the

country was accurate. Violence erupted in cities across the country in the wake of the assassination as bands of Negroes smashed windows, looted stores, threw firebombs, and attacked police with guns, stones, and bottles. Memphis endured six hours of looting, arson, and shootings on assassination night. Tennessee National Guardsmen helped patrol possible trouble areas as a dusk-to-dawn curfew was enforced.

Schools were nearly empty Friday as both black and white students stayed away. A vocal protest was sounded by several students at Claremont. Someone wrote in chalk, "Rejoice, the King is Dead" on the sidewalk in front of the school where student buses unloaded. Several Negro students reacted strongly to the display by shouting and milling around. Custodians quickly removed the graffiti. There was a brief shoving match between black and white female students.

The local chapter of the National Association for the Advancement of Colored People scheduled a memorial service at 3:00 p.m. on Sunday at the Civic Coliseum followed by a march on Gay Street in downtown Knoxville. I was forbidden to leave the house, or at least the neighborhood, for the entire weekend. There was scattered sniper fire throughout the city, and it was risky to venture away from home.

Brad called early Saturday and asked if I wanted to shoot hoops. I replied I was free after lunch. The weather was unusually cool, and we both wore jeans and long-sleeve shirts.

"That's pretty bad about Rev. King, don't you think?" he asked while making a fifteen-foot jump shot.

I rebounded the ball, shot a lay-up, and replied, "Yeah, it takes a really sick man to do something like that. The country is in turmoil."

"It's a sick society," he noted sincerely. "How about a game of HORSE?"

"You're on, but I go first." I realized if I didn't shoot first and make the shot and continue to make shots, Brad would put me out of the game straight H-O-R-S-E. He was that good.

I made a lay-up from the left side, and Brad responded with ease. I tried a jump shot from the right side and missed the basket as well as the backboard.

"Air ball!" he laughed, grabbed the ball, took a couple of fancy dribbles, and drilled a hook shot through the basket, barely touching the net.

I missed the shot.

"H," he shouted, taking the ball, and readying his next shot.

Brad shot from the perimeter and said, "Do you think your folks will let you go to the memorial service tomorrow? I want to go."

He missed the shot, and I grabbed the rebound. "Are you crazy? Not a chance. I'm lucky to get out of the house and come across the street. They wouldn't let me go to school yesterday. Mom's a basket case," I replied, missing the shot.

"We can sneak and go," he suggested, making a difficult turn-around jumper.

"No way. What's gotten into you? Do you value your life?" I shot and missed.

"O."

"Come on wimp, we haven't done anything daring for a long time." He made his shot. I missed.

"R."

"Nope. You're not talking me into doing something stupid again. The last time I was grounded for a week."

He looked graceful as he took a shot from twenty feet, and it sailed through the hoop. "When was that?"

"That camping trip last Summer when my folks thought we were at David Peterson's house, and he was so hung-over the next day that he puked all day and confessed to his parents about the trip and the beer. David told them who was camping with him, and they called everyone's parents. My folks were totally pissed and didn't trust me for months. I missed the shot, and he momentarily stopped playing.

"Our parents didn't know about the beer. They were upset about us lying about spending the night with David when we were with a bunch of guys camping."

"I know that, but mine said what if something happened to one of us, and no one knew where we were?"

"That's a chance we took, and if David could hold his beer, no one would have learned what we did. It was the chugging that did him in. We won't be able to pull that off again, and it was a blast camping and shooting the shit with the guys." He resumed the game.

"S." He made an easy lay-up, and I missed and accused him of breaking my concentration with the constant chatter.

"E," he laughed. "That's HORSE. Want to go again?"

"I'm first and quit talking so much. You're breaking my concentration!" I shouted.

"Not unless you agree to go. I've got an air-tight plan. Plus, remember you owe me for giving you and your pledge brothers a ride after initiation. I risked my life for you."

"That was a long time ago," I replied.

"Anyway, back to my plan for Sunday." Brad proceeded to detail his elaborate scheme whereby I'd inform my parents that he and I were going to 1:00 mass and staying for a CYO (Catholic Youth Organization) function afterward in the church social hall. We would be home for supper.

"Bro, they're not going to let me out on the streets, I'm telling you. People are getting shot."

Brad pleaded, "Will you at least ask? Better still, I'll ask. They're not as likely to tell me no as you. And no one's been shot in Knoxville."

I believed Brad was dreaming but decided to humor him. I assumed my parents were more likely to tell him no than me but didn't argue the point. They weren't his biggest fans, but he didn't know that.

"What about your folks? How do you know they'll let you go?" I asked.

"Oh, the whole church thing is real, but I don't plan to stay for the social."

"What if something happens and there's a riot or someone starts shooting? You've got to be kidding if you think there'll be many white people there."

"I assure you that the white people who are there will be respected for attending," Brad said convincingly. "The mayor and other white leaders are speaking. Nothing to worry about. I really want to go."

Brad had never shared feelings about Negroes or race relations with me. "Why is this so important to you? Why the sudden interest?"

"Attending the memorial service is the right thing to do. I've played sports with Negroes since junior high school, and I believe they'll appreciate my concern. I feel helpless sitting around all weekend and doing nothing. There's so much happening throughout the country."

"I still believe you're crazy, but we'll give it a shot. I know what the answer will be," I added.

Having convinced me to attend the memorial service, we played another game of HORSE, which I lost without Brad getting one letter.

My parents never ceased to amaze me. Not only did they grant permission for me to attend church and the social, they said it was a good idea for me to get out of the house since I'd been cooped up since Thursday. Church was a safe haven.

The mass dragged, and the priest's homily lasted fifteen minutes. I glanced at my watch throughout the service. Brad convinced me to leave after communion. He had driven his parents' car, and we quickly exited the parking lot and ventured downtown for the memorial service. We followed Interstate 40. We determined it was unsafe to take side roads, assuming that they offered better hiding places for snipers than the interstate. Slumped in my seat the entire route, I cautiously searched for snipers.

It was eerily deserted. We passed several State Trooper cars, which was a welcome site, and exited at the Civic Coliseum. We arrived at the parking lot, and everywhere I glanced, my view filled with black faces. My hands nervously shaking, I searched for white people but saw none. I was consumed with the thought that every Negro was staring at us and holding us responsible for Rev. King's death.

My voice shaking, I said, "I'm not sure about this. I've changed my mind. I believe we should go home. It doesn't look safe to me."

"It's cool. Don't be such a big baby. We came this far, and we're not going back now. I've got your back. We'll be alright. Trust me."

"You've said that before. I can't believe how many things you've talked me into, and this one takes the cake."

We parked and made our slow, hesitant trek into the building. My tension eased when I spotted several white people in the foyer, but I couldn't abandon the feeling that the Negroes glared at us with disgust. I suppressed the urge to offer apologies to the gathered crowd.

We entered the main hall and sat in a vacant row, not wanting to push our luck by sitting next to Negroes. Above the eerie quiet, a rendition of *We Shall Overcome* blared from an organ. Several individuals, including Mayor Leonard Rogers and a white man with a clerical collar, conversed on stage.

The lights dimmed, and a speaker approached the dais. Only the hum of the ventilation system broke the intense silence. The man stared speechless at each section of the room, collecting his thoughts, or perhaps for effect. The upper decks of the Coliseum were empty. With his head bowed, his low, yet commanding voice filled the void.

"Brothers and sisters, my name is Reverend James Crowther, president of the Knoxville chapter of the Southern Christian Leadership Conference. We are here today to mourn; yet, we are also here to celebrate. We mourn the passing, as well as celebrate, the life of a great man, the Rev. Dr. Martin Luther King, Jr. It is almost ironic," he paused to collect his thoughts and continued in a choppy, slow delivery, "that a man who spent his life preaching peace, should die so violently at the hands of a cowardly assassin." A chorus of "amens" sounded from the audience.

The speaker paused and struggled to find the appropriate words. "At this time, I call on Father Thomas McCoy, chair of the Knoxville Ministerial Association, for the invocation before beginning our program." The minister I saw with Mayor Rogers addressed the audience and asked us to stand and bow our heads. He proceeded to offer a five-minute tribute to Dr. King. It sounded more like a speech than a prayer, but I didn't sigh or dare show any sign of disrespect.

The prayer concluded and solemn music flowed from the speakers. The beat increased, and a gown-clad choir of Negroes climbed the stage steps and sang a rousing spiritual hymn. As they finished a second song, much of the audience was on its feet, singing, shouting, and waving hands. The mood was upbeat. Brad and I didn't want to stand out in the crowd, so we stood with everyone else and clapped our hands.

Rev. Crowther thanked the choir as it exited the stage.

Once the atmosphere returned to a quiet respect, he addressed the crowd with broken sentences but increased his delivery as his confidence and words won audience support.

"Brother Martin, can you hear us on this Lord's day? Are you finally at peace, my brother? You've gone to the mountain top and left us on this God-forsaken earth to continue the struggle you so nobly began. You've left your little children to bear the heavy cross against prejudice, injustice, and the ills of a decrepit society."

He paused and wiped his brow with a red handkerchief, which he carefully folded and returned to its place in his breast pocket. He sipped water and continued, "In this hall echoes the voices of George Washington Carver, Langston Hughes, Willa Cather, Frederick Douglass, Rosa Parks, Booker T. Washington, and Harriet Tubman. But those words are overshadowed by the powerful words of the man we honor today. Rarely have such words been delivered so eloquently and brilliantly. Never has one person gone so far and contributed so much to champion the cause of our people. Will there ever be another who sacrificed so much, including his life, to attempt to right the wrongs we have suffered for over 300 years?

"Over Easter weekend in 1963, Dr. King was jailed in solitary confinement for leading nonviolent protests against racial discrimination. In his famous *Letter from Birmingham City Jail*, he wrote, in part, 'Let us all hope that the dark clouds of racial prejudice will soon pass away and the deep fog of misunderstanding will be lifted from our far-drenched communities, and in some not too distant tomorrow the radiant stars of love and brotherhood will shine over our great nation with all their scintillating beauty.'"

He paused to allow the words to absorb, yet not long to keep from losing the captivated audience. With passion, he roared, "The radiant stars of love and brotherhood will shine over our great nation. Love and brotherhood. Where was love last Thursday night at the Lorraine Hotel? Where was brotherhood when the bullets struck and entered deep into his flesh? Who dares blast the sound of fury and cry foul at this repulsive act of barbarity? Where were the repressors when his little children asked why daddy wasn't coming home tonight?

"So cold is the wind that sweeps across our nation this day. The ugly violence that Dr. King bitterly opposed and resulted in his untimely death at a mere 39 years of age, has erupted throughout America. Our brothers are burning their neighborhoods and killing each other. We cannot let this be the legacy of our fallen leader. More coffins, burned-out shells of tenements, and tear-stained faces of young children cannot be his bequest. We must send a message. I said we must send a message!"

There were shouts of "amen" and "we must send a message!" People were on their feet.

Pounding his fist on the podium to emphasize his point, he shouted, "We must send a message--not only to our white brothers and sisters that the struggle did not end in Memphis, and that we shall overcome, but a message to our Negro brethren that we have only just begun to fight! Memphis is not an ending but a beginning, a beginning of another long march--a march through Birmingham, through Atlanta, through Watts, through Dallas, through Detroit, through Selma, through Washington, D.C., and all across the entire United States of America until we, too, can say with pride and jubilation: we have reached the promised land."

As each city was mentioned, the crowd repeated the words in unison. Rev. Crowther worked the audience into a frenzy. My nervousness returned, but it was no longer caused by fear of the present, but fear of the future and an unknown fate.

"Brother Martin said he may not get there with us, but with God as my witness, I tell you this day, that his spirit will guide us, his words and wisdom will create a path, his eyes shall shine like a lighthouse to provide a beacon, his blood will quench our thirst, and his shouts of *Free at last! Free at last! Thank God Almighty, we are free at last!* shall be etched in our minds forever as our motto, demanding freedom and justice... for all!"

I glanced at Brad, and much to my surprise, tears streamed down his cheeks. It was the first time that I saw my hardened and tough-skinned friend emotional, and I would never see it again. I was touched, and my respect and admiration increased. We never mentioned that private moment we shared.

The resounding applause was deafening. The audience jumped to its feet as Rev. Crowther waved and took his seat. The cheers of approval continued, and he rose and triumphantly saluted the crowd.

The program continued for another hour with other speakers, including the mayor, attempting, unsuccessfully, to steal the thunder of the audience won by Rev. Crowther. It was a thrilling and enlightening afternoon. I'm glad that I attended. It remained a secret, however, as both Brad and I feared our parents' wrath should they learn of our dishonesty.

No sooner had the violence and riots subsided nationally than another angry and demented individual, Sirhan Sirhan, crashed into the limelight and headlines by killing Sen. Robert Kennedy, who only moments earlier claimed victory in the California Democratic Presidential Primary. Within two months, the course of American history, and perhaps the world, was drastically altered by the selfish acts of two crazed men. What had our nation become?

The Supremes *I Hear A Symphony* played on the car radio as Brad and I followed the same route home from the service. We felt more at ease with the drive home. We reviewed the program, particularly Rev. Crowther's stirring eulogy. We survived the day without incident, and my parents never asked how my day went. Amazing.

Rev. King's death was still fresh on my mind, and I was not as deeply affected by Sen. Kennedy's death as I was by his brother's assassination; yet, in later years, my admiration for Robert grew to exceed that of John, and I dream about the potential greatness he offered the country and the world, particularly an earlier end to the Vietnam War.
In his tribute to his brother at his funeral at St. Patrick's Cathedral in New York City on June 8, Sen. Edward Kennedy said, "My brother need not be idealized or enlarged in death beyond what he was in life, to be remembered simply as a good and decent man, who saw wrong and tried to right it, saw suffering and tried to heal it, saw war and tried to stop it…As he said many times, in many parts of this nation, to those he touched and who sought to touch him: 'Some men see things as they are and say why. I dream things that never were and say why not.'"

12

Our sophomore year finally ended. It was a period that increased my maturity and cemented my stature with my peers. I made several sacrifices to build my self-esteem and develop friendships. Were they true friendships? I was unsure. Brad and I remained close, although he continued to spend more time with his fellow athletes and Kings than with me. Karen and I continued to date, but we didn't see each other as much because of our various commitments. I considered giving her my Royals pin at an appropriate opportunity. Skip and I were constantly together and regularly double dated. I'd always be there for Brad if he needed me, and I hoped that he would be there for me.

Approaching was the first Summer in which I had my driver's license. I anticipated three months of lounging at the lake, swimming, and water skiing, playing cards, and partying. My carefree dreams came to an abrupt halt one June day at supper when my father asked, "Steve, what kind of job do you plan to find this summer? You need to start saving for college."

I took a large bite of food to delay my response. "I haven't thought about it," I nonchalantly replied, hoping to end the discussion.

"Then you'd better," he shot back. "When I was your age…" he began.

"Here we go again," I interrupted, rolling my eyes.

My previous Summers' incomes were derived from mowing lawns and occasionally working for Mr. Erickson and other neighbors. I had a paper route for the *News Sentinel* in elementary school but did not save money.

"You might check to see if they need bag boys at Cas Walker's Supermarket," Mom contributed and added, "or ushers at the Kingston Pike Theater."

"How am I supposed to get there, ride my bike?" I asked sarcastically.

Mom and Dad glanced at each other, smiling. "Well, son, your mother and I may have a solution for that," he offered. My attitude changed, and I cut him off, shouting, "A car?"

"Perhaps," he said. "If you find a decent job that requires transportation, we'll look into buying a car for you."

I was excited, and suddenly the prospect of finding a job for Summer became more appealing. "Cool!" I exclaimed. "I know just the car."

"Hold on. Not so fast," Dad said. "Don't get your hopes up. We'll shop around for an older used car. That's all we can afford."

"But I'll have a job and will help."

"No, your money goes into the bank for college," Dad responded.

I spent the next two days visiting Cas Walker's Supermarket, Western Auto, the movie theater, the bowling alley, and other establishments along Kingston Pike. My late start at a job search was futile. College and high school students had taken the Summer positions. My frustration and despair mounted, and the outlook of getting a car dimmed. It should come as no surprise as to my rescue, who should appear? Brad!

"Hey, fart breath," Brad yelled from his house as I lounged in a lawn chair on our patio, contemplating my destiny. I turned and shot my middle finger. "Come here," he ordered.

"You come here," I said, ignoring his command. "You ain't my boss."

"I'll meet you halfway," he countered.

I paused, and compromising, met Brad on the street between our houses. "How'd you like to go to Gatlinburg for the Summer?" he asked.

"What do you mean?"

"We'll find jobs. I already have a place to live."

"What the hell are you talking about?"

"You honestly believe our parents will allow that? Your folks are stricter than mine."

"Here's the deal. Robbie Vandergriff and Ralph Carter found jobs and rented a chalet in Gatlinburg. They can't afford the chalet by themselves, so they asked if I want to join them. We need one or two more guys to make a go of it."

Robbie and Ralph were senior Kings, and the opportunity to spend Summer living with them was a dream come true. I jumped at the chance.

"How did they rent a chalet? They're not old enough," I asked.

"Robbie's parents signed for it. I'm surprised, but they're rich and they trust him."

"Where did they find jobs?" I asked.

"At a restaurant at the new ski resort. They're waiting tables. They said they can get a job for me, and we can ask if there is one for you."

Visions of living in a chalet in Gatlinburg with three or four guys, endless partying, and getting laid danced in my head. There were two major obstacles, however, my dad *and* my mom. I was convinced they would not allow a sixteen-year-old to leave home and live on my own, even if it was only an hour away. I also wondered what Karen would think about me leaving for the Summer.

Brad made his usual offer to present the case to my parents, but it first required that I carefully map a strategy to handle the plan. My parents were more likely to give permission if Brad's parents allowed him to go, and vice versa. If we both went, we would look out for each other. Hopefully, my parents realized that my local job search was in vain, and this was the last opportunity to locate work and save money for college.

Until the day I die, I'll find it difficult to believe that my parents agreed to my spending the Summer in Gatlinburg. It said much about the trust they held in me. I was young, and it was the first time that I would be away from home for a long period. I didn't sense having any difficulties or being homesick since I would be a mere hour from home.

My parents set several conditions, however. I had to forfeit buying a car because I was sharing rent and other expenses. I agreed to bank half of what I made. It was tough forfeiting the car, but I assumed it was a temporary sacrifice because I'd eventually get one. This was an opportunity too good to miss. Once I located a job, hopefully it would be close enough to walk to work or perhaps one of my roommates would provide a ride. I'd worry about that later.

I borrowed Mom's car the next day, and Brad and I traveled to Gatlinburg. We stopped at the chalet to visit Robbie and Ralph before they left for work. I was astonished upon entering the facility. I imagined an old, run-down shack, but the house was a year-old two-story, three-bedroom, two-bath dream home! I was in heaven, which increased the importance of finding a job, even if it was scrubbing toilets.

Robbie and Ralph arranged a job for Brad washing dishes at the restaurant where they worked, but there was nothing for me. Brad went with them to the restaurant to meet his employer and sign papers. I walked the streets for several hours, tramping from tourist trap to tourist trap searching for employment. I traversed both sides of the Parkway and finally reached its end at the entrance to the Great Smoky Mountains National Park. I stopped at Polly Bergan's dress shop as a last resort, hoping to find anything to do, and visited businesses along Highway 441. I was desperate. My blistered feet ached. My shirt stuck to my skin. I stopped at the Smoky Mountain

Market, the last business before leaving the city and entering the national park. I dropped a quarter in a soft drink machine and pushed a button. Nothing came out. I was hot, tired, and angry, and I kicked the machine.

"Hey, stop that!" a voice sounded. I turned and saw an apron-clad youth about my age approaching. He was slender and wore his blonde hair in a ponytail. He had a bright smile and appeared more friendly than angry.

"It ate my money," I said.

"Stupid machine. Hold on a sec," he said, taking a mass of keys from his belt and opening the machine, a slow and tedious process. "What do you want?" he asked after completing the task.

"Mountain Dew," I responded. He retrieved my drink. I pulled the pop top and flicked it in a garbage can. "Thanks."

"Think nothing of it," he smiled and turned to leave.

"You work here?" I asked the stupid question before realizing the obvious answer.

"Yep. My aunt and uncle own the market."

"Any chance of needing more help?" I asked without optimism, dreading the response.

"Maybe," he said. "There's only two stock and bag boys, and we're putting in a lot of hours. Now that it's Summer, the tourist trade has more than doubled. Where you from?"

"Knoxville."

"Oh, I thought you were an out-of-state tourist."

"Nah. I'm here for the day searching for a Summer job. I can't find anything."

"You started late. The college students grab everything before Spring quarter ends."

"I know. Some of my high school buddies have jobs at a restaurant at the ski resort and a place to live, so I'm desperate. If I spend the Summer at home, I'll go crazy."

"I know how you feel," he said. "I live with my parents in Sevierville and commute here every day."

Someone called from the market door, "Jimmy, we need you."

"Okay," he answered and beckoned me, "Come with me. I'll see what I can do."

We entered the market and walked to the office in the rear. "By the way, what's your name?" he asked.

"Steve Jackson."

"Hi, I'm James Madison, just like the president!" he laughed, shaking my hand. "Call me Jimmy." "What a nice guy," I thought to myself.

After a long, frustrating day, luck turned in my favor. I had a brief conversation and answered questions from Jimmy's uncle. Jimmy assisted my effort by convincing his uncle that more help was needed. His uncle offered a job and asked if I could start the next day. I responded that I needed to return home to pack clothes and move in with my friends. I started two days later.

Thus began the first time I lived away from home on my own. I learned lessons that would help me when I left home permanently. It was a Summer filled with both good and bad times, and one that left many memories.

The job was a boring pain. I stocked the shelves and bagged and carried groceries to cars, campers, and trucks. I wasn't supposed to accept tips, but I did on the rare occasion they were offered. The locals never tipped. I swept and mopped floors, dusted the stock and shelves, and chopped blocks of ice when someone wanted a half block. I once stabbed my palm with the ice pick, and the boss was angry because he had to throw away the entire block of blood-stained ice, a loss of a mere fifty cents.

As Summer progressed, we met other student

employees and entered an active night life of partying, drinking, and socializing. I was amazed at my newly found freedom. I came and went as I pleased. I went to bed when I wanted. I questioned if I could return home to endless restrictions and nagging at Summer's end.

There were several occasions I worked with a hangover or with few hours of sleep. I wasn't a huge drinker but joined the crowd, sometimes sipping the same beer for hours to appear social.

We developed a fear that our parties would be busted by the Gatlinburg police. They had a reputation for raiding student parties and citing violators for underage drinking or contributing to the delinquency of a minor. The offenders paid a cash fine and were released with an assurance of no permanent record. I wondered what happened to the cash. The police knew the merchants depended on the Summer help and they didn't want to antagonize them by harassing and arresting the student workers.

It didn't take long for the chalet to become trashed, considering we were four guys used to our mothers performing the household duties. In July, we gained a fifth roommate, Linda Thomas, Robbie's girlfriend, who couldn't bear being away from him for the Summer. She found a job making taffy at one of the numerous candy stores. Her parents assumed she was living with her older college student sister and two other girls who were working downtown. Once Linda moved in, we agreed to design a work chart and share the various chores. That worked for two weeks, and thereafter poor Linda fell into the role of cleaning and cooking.

I worked for two consecutive weeks before earning a day off. I was exhausted from working and heavy partying and planned to spend the day catching up on sleep. Brad and I shared the solitary room on the first floor, and I was sound asleep when suddenly I was jarred awake with the slamming of a pillow across the back of my head.

"Get up, sleepy head," Brad laughed.

"You son-of-a-bitch," I yelled angrily. "You scared the shit out of me. Go away. This is my first day off in two weeks and you woke me up at the crack of dawn!"

"It's 10:00 and the day's wasting. We're going tubing. Let's go!" He struck again with the pillow. My anger increasing, I grabbed for the pillow and felt it slip from my hands as he pulled it from my grip.

"Not fast enough for the Brad," he boasted.

I lay on my back and begged him to leave. "I'm dead, man. Go without me. I've got to sleep."

"Nope. It's a beautiful day and we don't know when we'll both have the same day off again, so up and at 'em." He attempted to swing the pillow again, but anticipating his move, I lunged forward and stole it, taking a swipe in his direction and hitting him across the back as he tried to duck the blow. He grabbed my foot and tickled it relentlessly until I begged for mercy and consented to go tubing. Tubing was like river rafting whereby we rented huge inner tubes and rode the rapids down the mountain creeks and streams.

"Shut the hell up down there," Robbie screamed from the room above, pounding on the floor. Brad and I looked at each other and chuckled. We weren't bothered by waking Robbie and Linda. There were several occasions we were disturbed by the squeaking bed springs and Linda's screams and moans from above.

Robbie and I didn't get along well. He called me wimp and often gave me a hard time. One day I was watching television in the living room, and he walked in.

"Hey, wimp, you never do any work around here. Linda has to do everything. You need to chip in with the chores." He towered over me.

I wanted to avoid a conflict and didn't respond. I was aware he didn't like me.

"Cat got your tongue?" he asked.

"I do my share," I said, short and sweet.

"That's a matter of opinion, and yours doesn't count much."

My anxiety increased as I saw that he wasn't going let the matter drop. "What got up your ass today?" I shot back.

"You don't scare me, pencil dick. You're just like the rest of the fucking lazy Royals. I don't know why Brad wanted you here this Summer."

I didn't want to continue the argument, and I knew he'd kill me if we fought.

"Go fuck yourself," I screamed.

"What did you say?"

"You heard me."

"I ought to beat your ass back to Knoxville."

Our argument grew louder, and Brad heard us in the bedroom and ran out.

"What the hell, Robbie! Lay off him," he said, face-to-face with Robbie. Brad was a foot shorter and 50 pounds lighter, but he stood his ground.

Silence. Robbie and Brad were in a staring contest. Robbie blinked first.

"I was just giving him a hard time. He's my favorite wimp," he laughed and walked toward the kitchen.

"What was that about?" Brad asked.

"I don't know. He's had a hard-on for me all Summer. Probably because I'm a Royal."

"If he bothers you again, let me know."

"I can take care of myself."

We borrowed Ralph's car and met Spencer, who worked with Brad, at the Mountain Spot where we rented inner tubes. It required two cars because we parked one car at the destination of our ride and the other at our origination point, in Elkmont. We carried the huge tubes to the water's edge. We were shirtless and wore old pairs of tennis shoes and cut-off shorts. I dreaded the first steps into the water.

"Damn, this water is cold," Brad exclaimed as he stepped into the mountain stream, pushing his tube forward. Even in the dead heat of Summer, the mountain streams ran cold.

"I dread this," I sighed, watching the other two brave the water. "Why don't I drive down and meet you two at the bottom?" I asked seriously. I was willing to bypass the expedition and take a nap in the car until their journey ended at the bottom.

"No way, chicken shit!" Brad said. "You're going down even if I have to tie you to your tube." I knew he meant it.

I slowly edged my way into the water, feeling the cold water rush over my toes, my feet, and ultimately my knees. Goose bumps rose on my arms. I turned and attempted to mount my tube backwards so I wouldn't have to get fully immersed. As I jumped up and pulled the tube toward my butt, it slipped out, flew into the air, and I fell to the creek's bottom, getting completely soaked. "Wow! It's cold as a witch's tit!" I cried, fighting my way to the surface. Brad and Spencer laughed. Spencer suffered the same fate, and the last laugh was on him.

It didn't take long to grow accustomed to the water as the hot sun beamed, eventually burning our heads and shoulders. I had gone tubing two or three times and enjoyed the thrill and danger of tackling the rushing rapids as they bounced my tube like a child's toy under the faucet of a filling tub. We were at the mercy of the gushing rapids that overturned an inner tube without notice and thrust its rider against the sharp and jagged rocks that lined the path.

There were points at which a rider who had fallen was engulfed by the rushing water, unable to compete against the force of the rapids that tossed and flipped with ease. A veteran tuber who fell continued to ride the rapids as best as possible, keeping his or her head high above water to avoid crashing into a boulder thrusting from the creek. A collision at high speed could result in instant death. Occasionally, a rafter died in this enticing sport, but the challenge and the fun continued to attract participants.

We paddled with our hands to push the tubes from the water's edge to the center where the rapids gained propulsion. When we reached that point, there was no turning back. Brad was first and I heard him scream, "Geronimo!" as his tube caught a rapid and began its journey. Spencer followed, and I was close behind because we needed to stay together and not get separated in case someone ran into difficulty and needed help, particularly if one of us fell and was separated from our inner tube.

There were sections where the water was calm and enabled us to catch our breath, capture a lost tube, or wait for tubeless stragglers, hoping they'd arrive uninjured. I'd suffered bumps, bruises, and cuts in the past and had fallen several times; however, I was fortunate to locate my tube and allow it to drag me to a calmer point. If I didn't stop my tube, I swam to safety and watched the tube's plight, hoping it would catch between rocks where I could retrieve it.

We were the only ones tubing at this location, perhaps because it was a weekday. Weekends found the creeks and rivers packed with tourists who weren't familiar with tubing, thus increasing the danger. The local and Summer residents knew the location of creeks off the main roads and away from pesky tourists. We agreed to challenge one of the off-the-beat streams on this venture.

The water was high, due to several days of torrential rain. I recognized and feared that we were in for a rough and potentially dangerous trip. I grasped both sides of the tube and let my hands grip the rubber from underneath, lest I suddenly be thrown off. I felt the rubber chaffing my arms as I gripped tighter, refusing to relent to the monster attacking me. I fought desperately to keep facing forward so I could see where I was headed, although there was nothing I could do to deter the spinning tube from its path. If I remained facing forward, I could attempt evasive action if necessary.

The tube swung around and steered backward down the rapids. I screamed from both the thrill and fear of the ride. I heard similar cries from my comrades. I bounced hard against a rock and felt the tube give, my shoulder slapping the slab as I spun forward again. I was nervous, but successfully maintained control thus far into the journey.

I grew tired and had difficulty with my vision because I could not release my hold and wipe the splashing water that continued to blind me. The first time I experienced tubing, I wore sunglasses, which was a mistake because they were lost in the rapids when I was ejected from my tube.

My arms hurt and grew weak from gripping the tube without rest. I no longer heard shouts from Brad and Spencer and couldn't locate them when my eyes momentarily cleared. My anxiety turned to fear at the same time I went over a rough set of rapids and bounced along the jagged rocks. I noticed a sudden drop in speed as the water fell to a smooth velvet. I risked letting go with one hand and wiped my eyes with the back of my fist.

"Hey, wimp! Where have you been?" Brad called.

"Jesus, what a ride!" I replied, paddling slowly to join Brad and Spencer at the water's edge. "Don't call me wimp!"

"Man, that was cool as hell!" Spencer said.

"I hope the rest of the way is like that," Brad added.

I was confused. My friends said it was fun, but I believed it was more dangerous than we expected. I had to agree with them or stay silent. I chose the latter. They didn't detect my anxiety. I wasn't in the mood to be abused because I realized we were only halfway through the ride. I had no choice but to continue because there was no exit from the creek at that point, and even if there was, I wouldn't quit and admit defeat. It had nothing to do with proving I had balls. It was purely peer pressure.

I sought a longer rest, but Brad's momentum was pumped, and he said, "Let's hit it." He paddled his way into the current, with Spencer and me close behind. I wanted to finish. I cursed Brad for forcing me to come and myself for giving in.

We quickly floated into the rapids. My arms continued to ache from the first ride. The adventure ceased to be fun. It became an obligation. It grew into a major ordeal to complete the course, and the constant threat of injury prevailed.

The sound of the water thrashing against the rocks drowned our screams. I spotted Spencer a short distance ahead but lost sight of Brad. He might be near, but the splashing water blinded me. We quickly raced against the driving force, and without notice, the water slowed. We reached another lull in the rapids, but it was too narrow and brief to stop and rest.

"This is great!" Brad shouted.

"It's the good life," Spencer agreed.

I remained silent, briefly exercising my arms, and attempting to ease the cramping. Exhaustion played a role in lessening my enthusiasm for the outing. My body was worn out from the previous week's activities. The current again took control of our fate and we drifted downward.

I heard it before I saw it. The waterfall's sound dominated the environs. It was a unique sound that blocked all other noise. I stole glances in all directions, hoping to spot a large rock or tree felled across the water to which I could grasp and stop my progress. I recognized eminent danger and needed to act quickly. There was nothing to stop my progress, and my speed increased as the path cut deeply into the ravine. I tightened my hold and attempted to remain facing forward to control the tube.

The noise from the falls increased. I prayed the drop would be short and safe. Spencer came into view, but I didn't see Brad. Spencer disappeared over the edge, and within seconds, I, plummeted over the falls into the depths below. I held onto my tube but bounced off as soon as it slammed into the cold water at the bottom. I sank and immediately struggled to the surface before hitting bottom.

I bobbed to the surface, spitting water, and gasping for breath. I searched for my tube and saw it slowly floating twenty feet away. I swam to retrieve it before it was captured by the current and forced downstream.

"Yippee!" cried Brad. "Man, that was unbelievable!" he said, retrieving and mounting his tube. "Damn, I want to do that again!"

"Where's Spencer?" I asked with concern.

"Has he come down yet?" Brad asked.

"I saw him go over before me."

"Don't shit me, man," he pleaded.

"I'm not kidding."

Shock overtook us and our eyes searched the area in vain. Brad paddled toward the middle to join me.

"I'm serious, Steve. Don't shit me," Brad said.

"I swear to God I saw him go over before me." Fear

engulfed me as I continued to search the immediate area and downstream. "Maybe he didn't fall off and kept moving downstream."

"No way," Brad interjected. "I would have seen him. It's impossible to stay on your tube once you go over the falls."

We heard the anguished cry simultaneously. On the far bank rested the prone figure of our fellow tuber. Brad paddled his tube to join Spencer while I swam, dragging my tube behind me.

"What's wrong?" Brad inquired with concern.

"I think I broke my fucking hand," Spencer replied in obvious pain.

"Don't touch anything," I warned Brad.

"I'm no fool" he shot back.

Spencer sat up. His left arm appeared normal, but his wrist hung freely and awkward. "My hand hurts like hell," he said.

"What happened?" I asked.

"I landed on it somehow. I don't know. It hurts like a motherfucker."

"What should we do?" I interjected.

"I'll go for help," Brad offered.

"Don't be stupid," Spencer insisted. "I can make it from here. We're almost to the car."

"How do you know?" I asked.

"I've run this course several times," he replied.

"Why didn't you tell us?" I asked.

"I knew you wouldn't come if you knew about the waterfall," Spencer confessed.

I glared at Brad with suspicion and realized without asking that he, too, knew about the falls. He was probably convinced I'd have doubts about tubing a creek with a dangerous waterfall. He was correct.

"Why are you giving me the evil eye?" Brad innocently inquired.

"You know why," I smartly replied.

"Man, I didn't know. I swear," he confessed.

"Liar," I accused.

Brad conceded the useless argument and asked Spencer, "What do you want to do?"

"I can make it. Seriously, guys, we're about 1,000 yards from the where the car is parked."

"Thank God," I sighed.

"I lost my tube," he added. "I'll have to piggyback with one of you. I can't grip with my hand. My tube should be at the bottom."

"Take mine, and I'll hang on to the back," Brad offered.

"You can't do that. You'll bust your balls on the rocks," I said.

"He's right," Spencer agreed and added, "We'll have to double up."

Brad held his tube in the shallow water and sat in the middle, his butt dragged on the sandy bottom. I helped Spencer to his feet. He sat on Brad. The two of them weighed heavy on the tube, causing it to remain in place. "Hold your wrist tightly to your chest and don't use it under any circumstance," Brad ordered.

"Lift up and push off with your feet," Brad encouraged. "We're stuck in the gravel and sand." I watched as they slowly drifted on the tube into deeper water and began the final leg of the journey. I remained several yards to the rear in case they ran into trouble.

Spencer's sense of direction was accurate and within minutes, we reached the bottom where we parked the car. We retrieved Spencer's missing tube and loaded two tubes in the trunk and tied the third to the roof. Our clothes were soaked, and we quickly changed into something dry.

We hurriedly drove to Gatlinburg's tiny general hospital. Spencer's wrist was x-rayed, which confirmed a bad fracture. Spencer was a minor and required to call his father at work to gain permission for an intern to place a cast on his wrist. Spencer completed several pages of paperwork, and we departed the hospital.

We attempted to make light of the situation but failed miserably. Brad and I kept apologizing to Spencer, and he insisted that we had done nothing wrong.

"It was just bad luck," he said. "Fate. It was meant to be."

"I know," Brad replied, "but it sucks. How can you work with that cast?"

"I don't know," Spencer sighed.

Spencer lived in Brentwood, a Nashville suburb, and attended Auburn. His parents were concerned about the level of medical care he received and desired a second opinion. They drove four hours that afternoon to Spencer's residence and returned home with him the following day to seek additional care. His injury prevented him from effectively waiting tables, and he notified his boss what happened and that he wouldn't return to work at the restaurant. Even if he could continue his job, his parents refused to allow him to return to Gatlinburg. I applied for his job and was hired on-the-spot since Spencer's sudden departure left them short-handed. His bad luck became my good fortune. I was thrilled to leave the market and join my roommates working at the restaurant but would miss my new friendship with Jimmy. His uncle was upset that I quit my job at the market and left them short-handed. Jimmy attended a few parties at the chalet, and we didn't lose contact for the remainder of our stay.

Summer dragged. The tubing trip became a faded

memory and I journeyed on several other tubing adventures. Brad begged to try the dangerous course again, but I adamantly refused to challenge the falls. After several trips, Brad and I proclaimed ourselves experts and bragged about our expertise and exaggerated about the ill-fated trip on which Spencer was hurt. The falls grew twenty feet higher each time we recited the story.

July became August and less than a month remained in our Summer excursion. School started the day after Labor Day, and we agreed to leave a week early so we could rest, take a vacation, and prepare for another year at Claremont High.

I worked late one night until closing at 2 a.m. By the time we cleaned the restaurant and I arrived home, it was after 3 a.m. I recognized the odor as soon as I opened the front door. I heard José Feliciano's *Light My Fire* blaring from the record player. I was tired, my heart raced, and all I wanted to do was go to bed. I closed the door and walked into the living room, adjacent to the kitchen. The room was dark and hazy with smoke. The only light was a black light and a lava lamp on the kitchen counter. Feliciano continued to sing in the background. A poster of Jimmy Hendrix glowed on the wall; Tide detergent painted on its edges glowing in the black light.

"Hey, Steve," someone called.

"Hey," I replied, recognizing Linda's voice.

"Come join the party," she offered.

I walked in saw people sitting in the haze but couldn't recognize anyone until I got closer. I searched for Brad. "Where's Brad?" I asked.

"At Trish's," Linda said. Trish was a waitress at the restaurant who regularly flirted with Brad.

"Have a toke, wimp," I heard a voice, saw a hand offering a joint, and realized its owner was Robbie. It was the late sixties, and drugs were prevalent everywhere. My classmates who considered themselves hippies were the only ones I assumed used drugs. I had yet to encounter a situation where drugs, particularly marijuana, were used. I had never tried marijuana and worried about the trouble we'd be in if the police busted the party.

"No thanks," I replied. I considered leaving but didn't have anywhere to go. Fatigue overruled, and I sauntered to the kitchen, took a beer from the refrigerator, and returned to the party. I knew it was useless going to bed amid the party noise because my bedroom was down the hall.

I drank two beers and eventually relaxed and enjoyed myself. The next time a joint was passed to me, I held it and debated whether to take a hit, and gave in, telling myself, "What the hell?" I sucked heavily and immediately coughed, my lungs rejecting the invading smoke. It reminded me of the day in the club house when I tried my first cigarette.

"Easy does it with Mary Jane," someone cautioned. "Take it in slow and easy and hold it in as long as possible and let it out slowly."

I followed the instructions with success and experienced my first marijuana high. I don't remember much more about that night because I continued to drink and get high. With little sleep, I awoke and vomited and suffered a horrible hangover. I was fortunate I didn't start work until 6:00 that night. I stayed in bed most of the day recovering. Brad didn't arrive home until late afternoon to shower before going to work. I debated whether to tell him about my previous night's experience, assuming someone at the party would inform him. I'm unsure how he would react, and I didn't really care. The matter wasn't mentioned. I'm not sure why I was ashamed that I finally smoked marijuana because everyone was doing it.

I worked longer than Brad that night, and when I returned home, I spotted a red bandanna tied to the doorknob of our room. It was a signal Brad and I established to warn the other that the occupant had company. This was the first time it was used. I smiled with satisfaction for Brad and realized that I was relegated to a sleepless night on the sofa. I thanked God we weren't hosting a party. I badly needed sleep.

I learned that Trish was Brad's overnight guest and she had given him a goodbye present. Brad was in the best mood I'd seen all Summer. He was jovial and chatted endlessly. Even though Brad bragged constantly about having sex, I never believed him. After witnessing his sudden happiness, I concluded that on one of the two nights he spent with Trish, he lost his virginity. He was subjected to endless harassment from our roommates, and I joined the reveling.

That weekend was our last two days in Gatlinburg. We planned to host a large bash Saturday night for our friends. I invited Jimmy Madison, realizing that I would probably never see him again, which was true. By the time I arrived from work, the party was in full swing. It was rowdy and loud and was an open invitation to the police. I heard the commotion as soon as I exited my car.

At 4 a.m., two police cars arrived, emergency lights off, to break up the party. Once the officers were spotted, several of our guests scrambled out the rear door and escaped up a hill behind our chalet. Their departure was unnecessary, however, as the officers merely ordered us to close the party and send everyone home. Summer was ending, and they didn't want the hassle of arresting and booking teenagers. They anxiously waited for the temporary workers and tourists to leave and another hectic Summer season to conclude.

Gatlinburg is now a distant, but fond memory. I learned to live independently, manage money, make appropriate choices (at least in my mind), and to wash (don't mix whites and colors) and dry clothes. My immaturity led to trouble with and fall from favor with Robbie, although I didn't care. I smoked marijuana a few more times but never experimented with other drugs. I continued to accept dangerous dares over the course of my life, including bungee jumping, cliff diving, and wild rides at theme parks and fairs.

    It was difficult to return home to restrictive parents and treatment conducive for an adolescent, a classification from which I believed I had graduated. My parents were tolerant and somewhat appreciative of my newly found independence; yet, they often reminded me that as long as I remained under their roof, I would abide by their rules. A compromise eventually worked, and they acknowledged that I had changed. I no longer was the young teenager who journeyed off on his own a mere two and a half months earlier.

13

I was pleased that I resigned my job before school started. I was exhausted and not prepared to resume the academic regiment. I slept twelve hours a day; a routine Brad shared. The next weekend, an end of Summer and farewell party for Skip was held at a friend's house in Cedar Bluff. Skip graduated, joined the Marines, and was assigned to Parris Island for basic training. I was surprised Skip joined the service because he was assured of a Vietnam assignment. Sandy cried endlessly following his decision. My romance with Karen cooled following my Summer in Gatlinburg, but I invited her to the party because she and Sandy were close friends. I concluded it best to take her rather than risk an awkward encounter at the party. Our reunion was pleasant, and I was pleased I invited her, but it was to be our last date.

Junior year. It arrived with far less fanfare than the previous year when I began high school. There was no concern about social clubs, social status, or athletic prowess. I continued involvement in the Royals, particularly attempting to better the club's image and entice a higher caliber of pledges from the sophomore class to join. My plan worked briefly but was later derailed by a group of agitated seniors who said the pledges were pussies and had it easy compared to what they had endured. When I eventually resigned my senior year because the members refused to eliminate hazing, I hoped it would send a message. I was not asked to resign, and I assumed many of the guys were relieved to be done with me and my rebellious suggestions. And to consider what I endured to become a member, only to abandon the club to take a stand. I stood alone, and it wouldn't be the last time.

I shared my frustration with Brad and told him that if the club didn't change, I planned to resign. He was stunned and gave me a hard time.

"I can't believe the shit you went through and you want to quit the Royals," he said. "All that crap for nothing."

"You just don't get it. I don't want anyone else to go through what I did. Sooner or later someone is going to get seriously hurt, or worse."

"I guess I understand, but you knew what you were getting into from the start. Just like I did with the Kings."

"I didn't know completely, and it was much worse than I expected. You don't understand. I don't want to see guys get the shit beat out of them. It's a matter of principle. If you knew up front that the Kings were going to put Nair in your hair and your crotch and pour Heet on your balls, would you have gone through with it?"

"That's hindsight. I don't know. It's done now. You made your decision, so you need to put it behind you. Be prepared for those guys to be pissed at you."

"Yeah, most of them won't care. I'm a pain in their ass. If they don't speak to me, I don't give a shit."

"And you wanted to be a King. You gave me shit and blamed me for you not getting a bid. I'm glad you're not a King and quitting the Kings."

"It's always about you, isn't it?"

"I'm sorry. Forget it. I didn't mean it."

"Yes, you did. Just fuck off."

Claremont had a Model United Nations student organization. They sent a delegation to the North American Invitational Model United Nations (NAIMUN) in Washington, D.C. every year. Our team was ranked one of the best in the nation and received the high honor of representing the United States at that Fall's gathering. The team prepared for months for the prestigious event. We were invited to send a second team to represent the African country of The Gambia, and we accepted; however, the club lacked enough members to fill the second team.

My American History teacher, one of the club's advisors, gave details about the Model U.N. and asked for volunteers to lead The Gambia delegation. I expressed interest and said I would ask my parents for permission and funds for the trip. I'd never been to Washington and jumped at the opportunity to visit the nation's capital.

My parents agreed to the trip, and our small delegation had much work to complete in a short time. Our small delegation was given five minutes for a presentation on the floor at the NAIMUN. It seemed like too much work for such a short appearance, but the speech was but a small component of the overall experience of attending the program and visiting Washington.

The added excitement for me was taking my first plane flight. I was nervous and slept little the previous night, dreading the flight. An hour into the trip, I puked in the barf bag and felt horrible. I was advised to purchase motion sickness pills for the return trip.

The ride from the airport to the hotel provided sneak previews of the monuments and sites we visited when our delegations didn't have meetings. I was in awe of Washington and felt like a child at Christmas. We stayed in the Shoreham Hotel, the most glamorous hotel I'd seen, much less occupied. I shared a room with three other classmates.

The Seventh NAIMUN convened in a huge ballroom the Thursday night of our arrival. Claremont's United States delegation, a member of the Security Council, attended the first session of the Security Council following the opening session.

General Assembly Nations were assigned to *blocs* according to the way they voted on issues. The Gambia was assigned to Bloc IV with 26 other nations. The blocs also met following the opening session. We were tired from the long day, and I struggled to stay awake. I listened to the proceedings, which were often tedious and boring. Our opportunity to speak was limited because of the large number of countries represented in the bloc. I was chosen to present on behalf of The Gambia and read prepared remarks I'd written after researching The Gambia at Claremont's library.

I went to the microphone and recited from my prepared remarks: "The Gambia is the smallest country on the African continent and was a part of the British Empire until *we* (I used the word *we* since we were supposed to be citizens from the country we represented.) gained independence in 1965. We are almost surrounded by Senegal, and our economy is supported by farming, fishing, and tourism. The population is less than two million. As an independent country, we are honored to be here with this esteemed body. Thank you for your attention." There was polite, obligatory applause, and I returned to my seat.

The Security Council and General Assembly Nations blocs met again following lunch on Friday. That morning we had embassy briefings and an Inter-Nation Simulation. Following our bloc meeting, we took a break to sightsee. Our rented bus took us to the Capitol, the White House, Arlington Cemetery, and the Lincoln and Washington Monuments. I became emotional at the Eternal Flame at the grave sites of John and Robert Kennedy. That horrible November day in 1963 remained vivid. I crossed myself and recited a brief prayer.

Saturday was filled with more meetings and the plenary session of the General Assembly. The NAIMUN banquet was held that night and keynoted by Great Britain's permanent representative to the United Nations, Lord Caradon (Baron Hugh Mackintosh Foot Caradon). We partied late into the night at the hotel and were warned by hotel security to be quiet and go to bed. I met a girl from a Catholic high school in New York, and we partied together. We maintained a correspondence until we graduated from high school.

The NAIMUN concluded on Sunday with closing remarks by Averell Harriman, United States diplomat and former New York governor, and the awards ceremony. Claremont's United States delegation won top honors. We had further sightseeing that afternoon, including the National Gallery of Art and the Smithsonian. The Smithsonian is so large that we barely made a dent in its offerings.

I developed a love affair with Washington and couldn't wait to return when another opportunity arose. I had never been so impressed with any place I'd visited, although I had not been anywhere that compared to this amazing city.

Before our return flight, I swallowed two Dramamine motion sickness pills I purchased at the hotel gift shop and slept the entire flight to Knoxville.

14

The remainder of Fall term passed quickly with only one major incident. I normally attended home football games with Karen, the Royals, or with Skip and Sandy. We journeyed to the Armory for dances that were held following the games. After one game in which we beat our rival, Fulton, 21-14, I was driving my parents' car with three Royals and turned to speak to one of them in the rear seat, and the one beside me suddenly yelled, "Hit the brakes!" I quickly glanced ahead and spotted a stopped car, waiting to make a turn. I swerved to the right to avoid a collision but was too late and hit the car's right rear bumper.

There was little damage, and I was pissed. We pulled our vehicles off the road to await the police. The clouds opened and poured rain, making an already bad situation worse. A car with two Royals stopped and offered help, but there was nothing they could do. I insisted that the three friends in my car ride with them to the dance. They were hesitant but agreed because I would be tied up with the police and no longer wanted to attend the dance. I knew that if I went to the dance, I wouldn't have fun.

I sat in the police car away from the rain while an officer completed the accident report. I received a ticket for failure to use due care and caution. I was nervous and dreaded returning to my car and driving home. The only thing I was pleased about was that it stopped raining as I slowly made the dreaded trip home to inform my parents. The encounter was better than I anticipated. They were happy that no one was hurt, and my dad helped ease my bad mood with his comment, "Shit happens!" We three went outside to inspect the car, which had a broken headlight and damage to the fender. Dad said he could get those replaced at a local car junkyard for little cost.

Winter passed and Spring 1969 arrived without fanfare. I anxiously anticipated my senior year. The guidance counselors advised rising seniors to begin preparation and register for the ACT and SAT as well as peruse college and university catalogs located in their office reception area. I planned to attend college, mainly to avoid the draft. I turned 18 my next birthday and was required to register for the draft; however, a new lottery system was implemented, and college and other deferments were eliminated. Brad, a year older, participated in the lottery and his birthday was assigned 248, a reasonably high and safe number.

Mother's Day, 1969. Dad and I took Mom to church and to Shoney's Big Boy Restaurant for lunch. It was a beautiful Spring day. The dogwoods were in bloom along Kingston Pike from the University of Tennessee to West Knoxville. Daffodils popped up in every available crack and crevice. I called Brad after allowing my food a couple of hours to digest and invited him for a jog. We shot baskets after returning.

Since it was Mother's Day, Dad cooked dinner, and I washed dishes. I retired to my room to complete homework and sat at my desk, studying, and listening to the Fifth Dimension singing *Aquarius* on my JC Penney transistor radio. I heard the phone ring, but not hearing my name screamed from the kitchen, I assumed it wasn't for me. I was bored and welcomed a break to talk on the phone.

The knock at my door startled me as I worked diligently to complete an English theme on Robert Frost's *The Road Not Taken*.

"Come in," I called.

Dad entered. I glanced at him but returned to my theme, pretending to be hard at work.

"May I interrupt?" he meekly asked.

"Sure," I replied, dropping my pen on the desk. I stared at Dad, but he refused to meet my eyes. I immediately suspected something was wrong.

"I've got bad news," he continued, his eyes glued to the floor, his hands clasped and rubbing. My thoughts raced. My grandmother suffered a heart attack the previous Fall, and the possibility that she died raced through my head. My sister lived in California. Perhaps something happened to her or my nephews. I waited without responding.

"We received a call (the phone call I'd heard earlier delivered the bad news), and I'm sorry to tell you, son, but Skip McDuffy was killed in Vietnam."

Silence. He awaited my reaction, but none came. I was numb with shock. I was devastated. He was the first friend I'd known who had died. The only other person I knew who died was my grandfather. He died when I was ten, which was years ago. We attended the funeral in Ohio, and I barely remembered it because I was young. I served as a pallbearer and recalled how difficult it was to help carry the heavy casket.

My voice quivered, and I fought back tears. "What happened?"

"His battalion was ambushed by enemy fire, and he was shot. They said he died instantly," Dad responded, his voice cracking as he delivered the details.

I wanted to know who called but didn't ask. I refused to ask further questions. I wanted to be alone. More silence. I prayed Dad would take the hint and leave.

"Are you alright?" he asked.

I nodded. He walked over and grabbed my shoulder with his right hand, giving it a tight squeeze. I felt his bony fingers. My shirt remained damp from his nervous hand once he removed it. He left the room and I broke into tears, muffling my sobs in my pillow to keep my parents from hearing me.

I read the account of Skip's death the following morning in the *Knoxville Journal*. According to the article provided by the Associated Press, "A Communist battalion attacked an American fire base east of the A Shau Valley and was repulsed. United States Marines joined South Vietnamese in an operation designed to trap 200 foemen (armed adversaries) south of Da Nang. Infantrymen of the 25th Division found an entrenched force of North Vietnamese southwest of Saigon and drove it into retreat in four hours of fighting. Paratroopers of the 101st Airborne were locked in a struggle described as 'eyeball to eyeball' on the slopes of a mountain called Ap Ba." Skip was one of several soldiers killed in the firefight. I stared at the newspaper article in disbelief for several minutes.

I was a pallbearer at Skip's funeral. I was honored that his parents considered that I was one of the six people closest to him. Sandy influenced the decision. I was devastated and relied on other friends to share and ease my grief. Even though Karen and I were no longer dating, we remained friends, and she was a tremendous help to me during this difficult time. My parents attended the funeral to support me in the most difficult challenge I'd faced in my youth, while giving me space and time to myself.

Murphy's Funeral Home handled the arrangements. I was glad it was a closed-casket service because I couldn't handle seeing Skip deceased. It was a military service, and several individuals in military dress were visible throughout. Hundreds visited to pay their respects and give condolence to Skip's family.

Sandy approached and took my hand. "I'm so sorry," I said.

"I know," she replied, wiping her eyes. "He thought the

world of you, Steve."

"I loved him like a brother," I struggled to respond, tears flowing.

"He felt the same." We hugged, and she returned to her family.

The most difficult part for me was at the cemetery when Skip was honored with a 21-gun salute. I held it together until the flag was removed from the coffin, precisely folded, and gently presented to Skip's parents, who were sitting adjacent to the casket. Our memories together flooded my head, and the realization hit me that I would never see my loyal friend again.

I didn't know where Vietnam was located. I assumed it was near China. I questioned why the United States was involved in a war that far away. I didn't care. Knoxville was part of the conservative South, and protests and civil unrest were relatively light. The University of Tennessee experienced demonstrations. The ROTC building near Stokely Athletic Center was burned. Students for a Democratic Society were active on campus and were blamed for the fire. They were a radical student group that utilized guerilla tactics to spread their anti-war message.

I hadn't paid attention to the Vietnam War, but now it had negatively affected my life. I was a victim of collateral damage. I lost my friend to a senseless and unexplainable conflict. Skip's death convinced me that the war was wrong and that I would refuse to go, even if drafted. I would flee to Canada. I would claim to be a conscientious objector. I would make every attempt to avoid the war. I refused to serve in a country whose location I couldn't find on a map.

I returned home with my parents and headed straight to my room. I wasn't hungry and refused supper, and my mother didn't force the issue. I was angry and fought the demons in my mind alone in my room, with only the sound of Bob Dylan's music breaking the silence. I sought a means to express my anger.

Skip was my friend. Perhaps I was his sidekick or the younger brother he never had. He was the big brother I never had. He helped me adjust to the rigors of high school, counseled me with humor when I was depressed, jokingly abused me endlessly, and was available whenever I needed him. The last time I saw him was at his going away party. We didn't correspond while he was in Vietnam. I'll always remember his gaping tooth smile, the already thinning blonde hair, the goofy southern accent, his skinny and lanky frame, his charming charisma, but most of all, I recall the friend who would do anything for anyone and was the individual who shared one of the most important events of my life. It seemed so long ago.

I mourned for weeks. I moped around the house, desiring sympathy, but getting none from parents who assumed I wanted to be left alone. Brad also kept his distance. He didn't know what to say. He hadn't known Skip as well as me, but realized he was my friend. I was pleased that he attended Skip's funeral.

Freedom from my gloom came the last week of school when I was invited to Big Ridge State Park on a senior outing with friends in the senior class. Sandy didn't go, and I admit I was glad. It would have been difficult for both of us.

We bused to Norris and by the time we arrived, I was my old self again. The highlight of the day was Tommy McCallister and me tipping over in a canoe and losing my shoes in the murky water. We searched the muddy bottom in vain for thirty minutes. My return home barefoot was cause for much banter on the bus, and I was glad I went. The laughter and friendship provided the therapy badly needed for my recovery.

Another Summer arrived, and once again I found

myself in search of a job. Gatlinburg was out of the question. It was impossible to save money with the costs incurred by another Summer in the resort city. I questioned whether my young body could endure another season of infinite abuse caused by endless partying.

With much regret, I ventured among the parade of shops, restaurants, and businesses in the strip malls along Kingston Pike. It was a futile search. No jobs were available.

I was angry to resort to mowing lawns but had no choice during what I expected to be a brief interim between mowing and locating a job.

15

My sister, Janie, her husband, Chuck, and two sons visited in late June. They made the long journey by car from La Jolla, California every two years to visit. My parents were ecstatic when Janie and her family visited. I shared my room with my two bratty nephews. It was an occasion when I couldn't wait to see them and later couldn't wait until they left.

Many of the highlights in my life, both good and bad, began with a phone call. The next event was no exception. The phone rang one day during Janie's visit, and Chuck, a district attorney, was notified that his assistance was needed post haste on a case that unexpectedly went to trial. Since he, Janie, and the boys drove to Knoxville, there wasn't enough time for him to return by car. It was necessary for him to return by plane.

"I'll fly home and take care of this trial business and fly back here to help drive across country," he said to Janie.

"I can make the drive with the boys," she insisted.

"You can't do that trip alone with those two," he challenged.

"Yes, I can. We'll stop more than we did coming out."

Chuck persisted, "No, I don't want you to make that drive alone. I don't feel comfortable with you making that trip alone with the boys."

"We can't stay much longer, and you don't know how long the trial will last," Janie persisted. "We need to get back because Charlie has camp in two weeks," she said, referring to her older son.

They paused to consider the situation. I sat, taking in the conversation, perhaps with anxiety, which I attributed to the thought of an extended stay by my nephews in my bedroom.

"I'll help you drive back," I offered, purely in jest, but assuming I had nothing to lose by making the offer.

Another extended pause while their minds pondered the idea, unknown to me and much to my surprise.

"That might be a good idea," Janie said.

"What do you mean?" Chuck asked.

"Steve can return with us and help drive, spend a week or two, and fly back. He's never been to California and will have a great time," she replied. She and Chuck attempted to coax my folks to visit for years. My parents rarely took vacations, and a trip to California was certainly out of the question. They claimed they didn't have the financial means to take vacations. I was the only person I knew whose family didn't take vacations.

My attention quickly turned to a dream-come-true trip to California. For many years, I desired to visit Janie and the West coast, but we couldn't afford the trip. Could it really be this close to reality and not mere coincidence?

"Will Mother and Dad approve?" Janie asked.

I didn't hesitate with my response, "No problem. If they allowed me to go to Gatlinburg alone last Summer, they'll allow me to go to California with you."

"Sounds good to me," Chuck said and added, "Let's make it happen."

....

"You're the luckiest son-of-a-bitch in the world," Brad said as we shot hoops the next day. "Thanks for deserting me in this God-forsaken place all Summer."

"You have the Kings," I replied with sarcasm.

"Screw them," he said without explanation.

"Too bad you can't go, too," I said, sinking a short shot from the foul line. My basketball skills had improved after shooting with Brad so much.

"You didn't ask."

I rebounded the ball, stopping the action, and held it

between my arm and my hip.

"You kiddin'?" I asked.

"About what?"

"About going."

"Hell, no."

I became excited about the possibility of Brad going to California with us. "Hey, man, I'll ask. There's room in the car, and you can help drive. Can you see the two of us on the beach with the babes in La Jolla? It's one of the nicest beaches in the world. We can learn to surf, party our asses off, visit Mexico, go to Disneyland, and live the life! What do you think?"

Without hesitating, he responded, "Cool, I'm in."

The possibility of Brad joining us on the trip was too good to be true. It took endless pleading with Brad's parents and convincing them that it wouldn't be a bother, and Brad wouldn't be in the way. Our luck ran true to expectation, and by week's end, we strapped ourselves into my sister's new 1969 Ford Torino, said goodbyes to tearful parents amid cautions to be careful, and headed West on Interstate 40 toward Nashville and Memphis. California, here we come!

Tennessee is one of the broadest states, stretching over 400 miles from East to West. We planned to drive to Arkansas the first day, but after seven hours, with stops in Cookeville, Nashville, and Jackson, and two fidgety boys, we were exhausted and decided to spend the night in Memphis. I had never been to Memphis, and I was excited to stop, although only for the night. Brad had driven through Memphis when he moved from Iowa, but they didn't stop.

Memphis State University was on my list of prospective colleges, but we didn't have time to visit the campus. We ate dinner at Silky Sullivan's in Overton Square and stopped at several businesses and night spots before returning to our motel. One place had a jazz band, and we listened to them play for a while. We were tired, and my nephews begged to leave.

We passed another establishment, and a sign in front read: Ink Spots Playing Nightly. "I can't believe it's the Ink Spots," Janie said. "I wonder if it's the original group?"

"What are the Ink Spots?" I responded.

"Not what are. Who are?" Janie corrected. "They're a band from Mother and Dad's era. I remember hearing them when I was small. Let's check it out." My nephews groaned with disappointment and begged to return to the motel.

"We won't stay long," Janie promised. "I want to see them and tell Mother and Dad that we saw the Ink Spots in person. They'll be impressed."

We entered the establishment and were immediately hit by the lingering smell of cigarette smoke and stale beer. The Ink Spots were performing, and Janie asked if we could stand in the rear and listen for a few minutes, and a waitress, who obviously was upset that we were not ordering anything, rudely responded, "Well, I guess so. Please don't block the exit."

One of the singers was canvassing the audience as he sang, stopping at several tables. "I need someone to come on stage and help me with a song," he said. Several hands flew up in the audience. Some patrons shouted and volunteered their friends, who sank from view in their seats.

The singer's canvassing drew him closer to us, and as he neared, my nephews pointed toward Janie and chanted wildly, "Take her! Take her!" She attempted to quiet them and stepped back, but her actions further encouraged her sons. The singer stopped abruptly and took Janie's hand, leading her toward the stage. She struggled to free herself, but his persistence won, and she trudged behind him, shaking her head, and covering her face with her other hand.

They reached center stage, and the singer asked her

name and where she was from.

"Let's welcome Janie Clark, all the way from La Jolla, California!" he announced, and the audience responded with applause. "We're going to sing a song called *If I Had A Hammer*. Do you know it?"

"I think so," Janie said, blushing so deeply that I saw her color change from where we were standing.

The music started, and the singer sang, "If I had a hammer..." He paused and encouraged Janie with his hand. They both continued, "I'd hammer in the morning."

The four of us howled and cheered. My nephews' exhaustion suddenly disappeared.

"I'd hammer in the evening. All over this land."

The lead singer backed off and left Janie alone. She continued the song, "I'd hammer out danger. I'd hammer out a warning. I'd hammer out love between my brothers and my sisters. All over this land." She realized she was singing alone and paused.

"Keep going, sister! You don't need us! You're a pro!" the lead singer exclaimed.

Janie shrugged and said, "What the heck?" and began the second verse, "If I had a bell..."

She concluded the song and received a standing ovation from the audience. She blew kisses and ran from the stage. She didn't stop until she grabbed her sons' hands and abandoned the club into the street and the night. Brad and I chased close behind with the lead singer's "How about that? How about that? A star is born!" fading in the background.

We had a good laugh about Janie's stage debut, and it brought admiration for my sister, whom I didn't know well. She was cool.

I wanted to visit Elvis's Graceland, and Brad wanted to see the Lorraine Hotel where Rev. King was killed the previous year, but Janie said we couldn't take the extra day for sightseeing. We had to get an early start in the morning.

The next day we crossed the Mississippi River into West Memphis, Arkansas. It was the furthest West I'd been, and the remainder of the trip would be new territory for me.

We drove through Little Rock to Dallas, and by the time we reached Dallas, I regretted agreeing to the trip. My nephews were driving Brad and me crazy with their constant bickering. Brad felt like an outsider but did well in keeping the two boys occupied with various games and activities. We spent the night in a Holiday Inn.

Brad and I took a walk after dinner for a break from my nephews. We were several blocks from the hotel when a thin, sleezy woman, scantily clad in a tight leather mini skirt approached us. "You boys want a date?" she asked.

Brad and I exchanged puzzled looks. We stared without responding.

"What d'ya say, boys, how about a date?" she repeated.

I didn't know what she insinuated, but Brad did. "How much?" he asked.

"Twenty-five for everything. Ten for a blow," she picked at her long fingernails as she sounded the response she'd given hundreds of times.

"Let's go for it," Brad whispered to me.

"Is she a hooker?" I quietly asked.

"Of course, stupid. What do you think she is, the mail lady?"

I stuttered, "You've got to be kidding. It may not be safe in this area, and you don't know what you might catch from a prostitute."

"I'll go only for a bj, man. You never know when you'll get a chance like this again."

The idea raised red flags. "Seriously, Brad. This is bad.

It doesn't feel right."

"But it'll feel good!" he laughed.

The woman was getting impatient. "How 'bout it, boys? I don't have all night."

"Where do we go?" Brad asked.

"Right behind us," she pointed to a dilapidated building. A sign above the door read *Thunderbird Hotel, Rooms by the Day, Week, or Month*. "Room's ten dollars," she added.

"That's twenty bucks," I said.

Brad removed his wallet from his pants, fingered a $20 bill, and handed the wallet to me. He also removed his watch and placed it on top of his wallet.

"What are you doing?" I asked.

"Just being careful," he said nervously. "You never know." The hooker laughed and continued to pick her nails.

"Man, you're crazy. I'm begging you, please don't go. What am I supposed to do?"

"Wait here."

"Is it safe if I wait here?" I realized there was no way to talk Brad out of this ridiculous act. I worried about him going inside the hotel alone with the woman.

"Sure. Just hang here and wait for me. You'll be fine." He turned and smiled at the hooker. She returned the smile, took his arm, and they walked to the hotel. The building's entryway was glass, and I watched them stop at the front desk, ascend a staircase, and disappear. The building was eight stories, and my eyes searched the rooms, waiting for a light to brighten a darkened window.

I realized I was asking for trouble standing alone on a street corner in Dallas after dark. It was not a safe situation. What if a cop saw me? Undoubtedly the cop would stop and inquire why a young white kid was standing on the street alone.

Seconds seemed like hours. I peered at my watch, realizing that only minutes had passed since I last checked the time. I worried that Brad might be dead with his throat slashed somewhere in the Thunderbird Hotel. Amid my worry, however, was a jealousy that Brad had the nerve to go with the prostitute and I didn't. He would brag to the Kings about this venture, most of whom wouldn't believe him. Afterall, he was only sixteen and wouldn't turn seventeen until the Fall.

I passed the time and amused myself with crazy thoughts. I wanted to kick myself. A rare opportunity, and I let it pass. I considered entering the hotel in search of the pair. "Perhaps we could go two on one?" I joked to myself, searching my surroundings for imminent danger. Brad and I did almost everything together, so why not this? I laughed at the idea, aware it was a stupid thought.

I was approached by another hooker during my wait, and I politely but firmly declined, hoping I wouldn't be mugged. "Janie will kick my ass if anything happens," I said aloud.

Fifteen minutes, which seemed to be an eternity, passed, and Brad reappeared, his head hung low.

"How was it?" I asked with excitement.

"Okay."

"That's all? Just okay?"

"Yeah."

"Don't leave me hanging like that. I want to hear everything," I pleaded with adolescent interest.

I realized that Brad's excitement converted to embarrassment.

"Let's get out of here," Brad said, walking in the direction of our hotel.

I again demanded details. "Not until you tell me."

"Okay, already, but let's go."

As we walked, Brad discussed his brief encounter with the hooker. "I paid for the room, and we went upstairs to this dumpy little cubby hole with a bed, a dresser, and a bathroom. She told me to sit on the bed, and she asked my name and how old I am.

He paused as we stopped to wait for a red light. "This is embarrassing," he shook his head.

"Since when do you care about anything?" I asked, laughing.

"Yeah, I don't know why, but it is," he said, before continuing, "She actually was nice."

"You're kidding?" I laughed.

"No."

"Did you talk about anything?"

"No, what would we talk about, the weather?" He laughed. "So that's it. Nothing more to tell." He paused and added, "There, are you satisfied?"

"Yeah," I said in disbelief at Brad's latest antic.

We reached our hotel, and Brad grabbed my elbow. "Do me a favor," he said, somewhat tense.

"Yeah?"

"Don't tell anyone."

"Why? The Kings will get a hoot when you tell them the story."

"Seriously. I don't want anyone to know. Promise?"

"Not until you tell me why."

"Okay. I shouldn't care, but I know that the Kings and my jock friends will never let me hear the end of it. It'll spread like wildfire throughout school, and I'll have trouble getting dates when they know that I was with a prostitute. Do you understand?"

I hesitated and knew he was right. "Yep. I know where you're coming from. You'll catch endless shit. Mum's the word. You can trust me, but you owe me big time, and don't forget. You always conveniently forget when you owe me a favor," I cautioned. He didn't respond, and I added, "When we get back, you should go to the health clinic for a screening," I cautioned.

"No. You can't catch anything from a bj."

"I wouldn't be so sure."

I could tell that Brad was irritated and tired of the conversation. "Let's drop it. It never happened. You promised. Let's hit the hay. I'm dead tired, and we have a long drive tomorrow."

We never mentioned that evening again.

The next day we tried to convince Janie to detour through San Antonio so that we could visit the Alamo and the site of the previous year's Hemisfair, but she said that we didn't have the time to spend an additional day the side trip would require. Driving Interstate 10 dragged endlessly for hours. I didn't believe we would ever get out of Texas. It seemed to take as long to cross Texas as the rest of the trip combined. Everyone had enough driving for one day, and we stopped in El Paso for our third night of the trip.

We hadn't reached California, and the trip thus far allowed me to appreciate that Janie and her family completed this cross-country trip every two years to visit. It was a challenge, particularly with two young children. It was bearable for me because of the beautiful sites on the way and visiting states for the first time. Although he wouldn't admit it, I presumed Brad was going crazy trapped in the car for four days without exercising. I promised him it would be worth it.

My excitement increased once we reached New Mexico. I have no idea why it was always one of my favorite states. I admired their license plate. The bright tag with the stylized red sun, symbol of Zia pueblo of Indians, on a yellow field, was colorful and attractive. I finally visited The *Land of Enchantment* and its endless desert and cacti. We stopped in San Fidel to take a picture of Brad and me standing in front of a twelve-foot cactus.

One more state to go before reaching our destination. We drove five and a half hours to Tucson and stopped for lunch and gas. We continued for another four and a half hours to Horseshoe Bend and decided to spend another night, even though we were only three hours from San Diego. We attempted to convince Janie to finish the trip, but she insisted we stop, get an early start, and arrive in daytime.

We finally arrived in California after four and a half draining days driving across country. Following the boring trip across Texas and New Mexico, I was unimpressed with the West, but Arizona's desert, amazing mountains, and tall cacti changed my opinion. We crossed into California past the agricultural check point, and I felt the energy surge in my body. My dream of visiting California arrived.

The dream was confirmed once we reached La Jolla. I was in heaven. I saw palm trees as well as the Pacific Ocean for the first time.

I had seen pictures of Janie's house, but it was much nicer in person. Brad and I shared a room. There was a pool, where Brad and I worked on building deep, golden tans, and a game room, complete with a pool table. Brad's excitement exceeded mine. "I can get used to this," he remarked after viewing the pool. I reminded him that the long drive was worth it.

Brad and I were two teenagers antsy to visit California for the first time. We enjoyed Janie and Chuck's sightseeing tours to the beach and other sites of interest in and near San Diego, but we longed to venture on our own. In walked Chad

Beaumont.

Chad fit his name. He was a hip, California surfer dude with long, sun-bleached hair. He was seventeen and lived in Janie's neighborhood. Janie sensed our boredom and invited Chad to meet us. Following Janie's introduction that we were from Tennessee, Chad responded, "Cool, dudes," and gave us a rounded clasp versus normal handshake. I chuckled and immediately admired our new friend.

"You dudes up for surfing?" he asked.

"Are we!" Brad jumped at the opportunity.

"Cool, let's do it," Chad said.

Brad and I were pleased that we built a good tan base because we didn't want to be white as ghosts when we arrived at the beach and appear to be tourists. We informed Janie that we were going to the beach with Chad and piled into his late model Volkswagen bug, surfboard strapped to the roof. Janie warned us to apply sunscreen and said that if we suffered a bad sunburn, it would ruin the remainder of our visit. We weren't familiar with the intense California sun.

We arrived at the beach, parked, and walked to Bearded Jerry's Surf Shop to rent two surf boards. I was surprised at the weight of the board and stopped several times to rest and switch my board position before reaching the beach.

Everywhere we looked were bikini-clad babes. I'd never seen so many beautiful girls in one place in my life.

"Jesus, Chad, how do you survive here?" I asked. "This is heaven!"

"Yeah, you grow used to it," he laughed.

"I don't know if I can," I said. "What a lifestyle. Surfing. Beaches. All these beautiful chicks. I'd flunk out of school."

"That's why I'm in Summer school," Chad added with a smile.

"You need to teach us how to surf," Brad interrupted, slapping his board.

"It's simple. You'll learn best by trying and trying. You'll fall off a dozen times before you get the knack of it," Chad noted as we walked to the water's edge. He held his board in front of him and continued, "Lie on it and paddle out with me. Be sure to paddle when there are no waves, and when a wave comes, just ride over it, but paddle quickly afterward or you'll be pushed back to shore. Once we're out far enough, mount your board and sit on your knees, facing the shore. Hold onto the sides and look back for the next big wave. As it reaches you, paddle like hell and ride the surf. As soon as you can, stand carefully and maintain your balance. Keep your knees bent and use your arms for balance. It's a breeze!"

He finished his instructions and began paddling away from shore. Brad and I raced to join him. I had trouble staying on my board as I fell off when the first wave slammed into me. I remounted and paddled to catch up and held on tightly as each wave approached.

"Okay, hillbillies, show me what you got!" Chad joked as he pulled himself onto his board and sat on his knees. I saw a huge wave approaching and jumped on my board and turned to watch the wall of water. As the wave neared, I paddled furiously and grabbed the sides of the board to keep from falling off. I rose to one foot on the board, keeping one knee down to maintain balance. Good so far. I lifted the other knee and planted both feet on the board, keeping my body in a squatting position. As soon as I let go of the board and tried to stand, I lost my balance and turned a somersault backward into the brink.

I fought my way to the surface, coughing and spewing saltwater from my mouth. I searched for my board and realized the surf took it to shore. I fought the heavy waves to retrieve it.

"Man, you're crazy to come up that fast," Chad chastised.

"Why?" I asked.

"Good way to get hurt. That board will ride high in the air and conk you in the head when you jump up like that. Give the board time to come down."

"You didn't tell me!" I shot back.

"Sorry." His sarcasm was evident.

Brad suffered a similar fate and fell on his first attempt to stand. "Damn, that was fun!" he declared, spitting salty saliva into the water. "Let's go!" He ran back into the water without waiting for us. My request for a longer rest was ignored, leaving me to race to catch the pair.

A dozen attempts later, I was exhausted and frustrated from my inability to stand on my board longer than ten seconds. Chad cautioned me to be patient, but I grew jealous of Brad's quick adaption to the board. He conquered the sport and rode a wave into shore before day's end.

After four hours of surf, sun, and fun, we called it a day. Overcome with exhaustion, I struggled to carry my board to Bearded Jerry's. I slept better that night than anytime I could remember.

Chad became our savior and stopped by or called daily to inquire what we wanted to do. Before our small vacation ended, my surfing improved, and I successfully made it to shore a few times without falling. It was exhausting but exhilarating. Brad and I joined the beach bum crowd, spending several days on the beach, dreading the day we were forced to return to Knoxville. Chad took us to parties and cook-outs on Shelter Island in San Diego and to Manhattan Beach. We spent a day hanging out at Balboa Park. I was enthralled with the hippies and flower children, and discovered a new favorite musical group, Vanilla Fudge. The environment contrasted sharply from Knoxville. We were in a new world we never dreamed existed.

"I wish more of our friends could share this experience," Brad noted as we soaked in the amazing atmosphere in Balboa Park.

"I agree. They would have a blast. They won't believe half the stories we tell them," I responded.

"It's going to be tough adjusting to that bullshit life in Knoxville. Football practice already started, and coach is pissed I'm not there."

"Maybe we don't go home."

"Don't temp me. I dig this lifestyle, but it's a stupid conversation because it ain't happening." He was sincere. He stared at the surroundings. He possessed a free spirit. In La Jolla, he had no reputation to live up to and no agonizing daily routine. Was this his true self? It was a moment I'll never forget.

Janie didn't want us to waste the entire trip on the beach and partying at night with Chad. She insured that we received a taste of culture with trips to the San Diego Zoo and the Salk Institute. One of the highlights of the trip was a Sunday spent at Disneyland in Anaheim. I wanted to go to Disneyland since I was a young boy, and it was another dream fulfilled. I was a movie buff, and a day trip to Hollywood provided excitement and anticipation that I might spot a famous movie star. We went to Graumann's Movie Palace, and Brad and I took turns fitting our hands and feet in the stars' cemented hands and footprints.

The time passed quickly, and Brad and I grew disappointed that our amazing Summer in California was nearing its finale. We were somewhat homesick, but a second consecutive Summer away from Knoxville helped affirm our independence and break from home.

Of historical note during our visit was the moon landing by astronauts Neil Armstrong, Edwin "Buzz" Aldrin, and Mike Collins on July 20. Janie and her family, Brad, and I were glued to the television as Armstrong took man's first steps on the moon's surface and said those famous words, "That's one small step for man, one giant leap for mankind." I never perceived that this would occur in my lifetime, although President Kennedy predicted the U.S. would journey to the moon before the end of the decade.

The only item left on our bucket list that I'd yet completed was to cross the border into Mexico. Janie hated Tijuana, and Chuck said it was unsafe, and I accepted that one goal would be unfulfilled. Brad and I refused to abandon the idea, however, and we predicted it would be easy to convince Chad to take us.

Chad welcomed the opportunity to escort us to Tijuana, but Janie and Chuck were hesitant to allow three young teenagers to venture to Mexico alone. Janie knew how badly we wanted to go and convinced Chuck to consent, but we first endured a twenty-minute lecture on the dangers of the Mexican tourist trap.

"Remember the laws are different," Chuck cautioned. "If you get into trouble, it will be difficult to help you. Foreigners have rotted for years in Mexican jails. They hate gringos. They love your money, but they hate you."

Chuck continued his advice, "I know you two are smart, but Chad can be foolhardy sometimes. Don't venture from the main drag. Guard your wallets. Put them in your front pocket. Whatever you do, don't bring any contraband back across the border. The U.S. Border Patrol will flag you to the side and search your car. I've heard they've cut people's upholstery, searching for drugs. There's no drinking age in

Tijuana, but don't do anything you're not supposed to do. Someone might put something in your drink and drug you. They'll take advantage of you at every opportunity. It's not safe, guys. Let me warn you, have a good time, but please be careful."

We chuckled at that last remark. If Chuck attempted to scare us into not going, it didn't work. The sermon ended, and we piled into Chad's VW and drove South to Mexico.

We enjoyed the sites without much conversation, and out of nowhere, Brad said, "Chad, have you ever been skydiving?"

"No, man," he replied. "I ain't jumpin' out of no plane."

"Me either," I replied from the rear seat.

"I really want to go." I wish we could find a way to pull it off out here," Brad insisted.

"Ain't happening. For one, we're too young, and two, it's expensive as hell. None of us have that kind of money," Chad retorted.

"Yeah, you're right," but I'm going to do it one day. Just wait and see."

We crossed the border into Mexico. I was stunned at the difference between the two countries. I visited impoverished areas in East Tennessee and Kentucky but never imagined such contrasting conditions in a matter of miles and minutes.

Tijuana reminded me of a Mexican Gatlinburg. There were tacky shops everywhere and countless people, particularly children, hawking everything from velvet paintings to ceramic bullfighters and bulls, to numerous religious relics. Chad warned that the vendors asked twice as much as they wanted, thus resulting in a bargaining game for a fair price. I bought a small velvet painting of a bullfighter for $15 that started at $30. It was a tough choice between the bullfighter and Elvis. I believe that I got a steal, but Chad laughed and said I could have bought the identical painting in San Diego for $10. I didn't care because I purchased it in Mexico. I planned to give it to my parents as a present.

"Hey, Chad, do you think we can buy some Spanish fly?" Brad asked about the aphrodisiac as we fought our way through the street-filled stands of continuous junk.

"What do you plan to do with Spanish fly, gringo?" Chad responded.

"Take it to Tennessee," Brad replied.

Chad laughed and answered, "You plan to get lucky?"

"You never know. A little Spanish fly can spruce up the occasion."

"Dude, you're crazy, but we'll see. I wouldn't trust anything you buy here."

The conversation was overwhelmed by loud Calypso music pouring from a corner bar, the El Cid.

"Let's check it out," Chad shouted.

I was hesitant and responded, "Is it okay?"

"Sure, why not?" Chad replied.

"Remember what Chuck said. He warned us to stay on the main drag," I warned.

"He worries too much," Chad insisted as he entered the western style swinging doors. Brad and I followed into the crowded and noisy, smoke-filled tavern. The atmosphere was flowing with partying locals and tourists. A mariachi band played while a Flamenco dancer in traditional dress danced and snapped her castanets.

"What do you want, dudes? I'm buyin'," Chad shouted over the noise.

"Margarita," Brad yelled.

"And you?" Chad poked his finger into my chest.

I hesitated, Chuck's warnings ringing in my ears. "What the hell, you only live once," I said and shouted "the same" to Chad.

Chad returned with three large glasses of frozen margaritas. The salt was caked on the glass rims, and the tequila permeated the air. I sipped my drink. "Wow, that's good," I said, licking salt from my lips.

"Here's to the best Summer of my life," Brad said, clinking his glass to Chad's, then mine.

"And to the coolest hillbillies I know," Chad added, repeating the clinking.

"And to the coolest surfer dude we know," I chimed in.

The tequila shot through our blood, and after Brad and I bought a round of drinks, we were tipsy. It was the first time I'd drunk tequila. Thus far I'd ignored Chuck's many warnings.

"I've got to piss like a wild racehorse," I said, and added, "I don't want to go to the bathroom alone. Someone go with me."

"Do you need someone to hold it?" Brad laughed, a bit intoxicated.

"If you can find it," Chad added with ridiculous laughter. Chad slapped Brad on the shoulder, and I shook my head in despair. I really had to pee.

"I'll go, I need to piss, too," Brad offered.

"Hurry back, girls," Chad chided as we walked toward the bar's rear.

The sign read *Caballeros*. We knew it was the men's restroom because men were entering and exiting. We opened the door, and a Mexican pushed us back, chattering in Spanish and waving his hands toward a stall in the bathroom. I glanced inside and spotted a toilet overflowing, water flooding the floor.

"But, but...I've got to pee badly," I pleaded, grabbing

my crotch.

The Mexican continued his endless chain of Spanish, pushing us and other men with both hands back through the door.

"Shit, man, I'm about to piss my pants," I said in anguish.

"Let's go out there," Brad pointed to an open door, leading to an alley.

I followed without question or hesitation. As we relieved ourselves against the rear wall of the bar, the pain eased in my groin. "You can flip it. You can flop it. You can bang it on the wall, but you gotta put it in your pants to make the last drop fall!" I recited as I zipped my fly.

"Paren!" I heard the command, which caused me to jump and turn toward the voice. I found myself face-to-face with two uniformed policemen.

"Let's get back inside. Hurry!" Brad shouted. We sobered quickly.

"Paren!" The shout, which we didn't understand, came again.

"Sorry, but the toilet was broken," I said slowly, hoping the two might understand if I spoke slowly. We were caught urinating in public. I panicked. Chuck was right. Brad and I will rot in a Mexican jail.

"Ustedes dos. Deténganse! Quedan arrestados!" an officer continued.

"Let's make a run for it," Brad suggested.

"No, they might shoot us," I replied, visibly shaking with fright.

"Ustedes vienen con nosotros." They motioned for us to follow them and took us by the arm.

"Do you speak English?" I asked. They responded another command in Spanish.

"We're up shit creek," Brad cried. This was the first time I'd ever seen fear in Brad.

I was struggling for survival. "We need to get our friend," I pleaded, pointing toward the bar. "Uh, mi amigo," I added, touching my finger to my chest, and pointing toward the bar.

The Spanish response was incomprehensible. "Shit, man, we can't leave without Chad. He won't know what happened to us," Brad said, his voice shaking.

One of the officers tugged my arm, and the other pulled Brad's. "Don't give them a reason to do anything," I cautioned Brad. "Shit, why didn't I take Spanish instead of French?" I questioned aloud.

The two officers continued their conversation as they led us down the alley. I envisioned us spending the next twenty years abandoned in a Mexican prison. Chuck's prediction came true. My family would never know what happened to me. I saw an international incident created over the issue. I became Walter Mitty, a character from a James Thurber short story, *The Secret Life of Walter Mitty,* that we read in English class.

Our stumbling trip down the alley resembled the last trek of a prisoner on death row. Only the *Bible*-reading chaplain was missing.

"Wait! Esperen!" We heard the shout and turned to see Chad racing toward us.

"Cuál es el problema?" Chad said in perfect Spanish.

"Estos gringos están orinando en público! Los gringos no van a tratar nuestro país asi!" came the response from one of the officers.

"Estúpidos gringos!" Chad laughed. "Crazy Tennessee hillbillies!" Chad circled his finger on his temple. The Tennessee hillbillies part we understood.

"Bueno, senores. Cuánto quieren?" Chad asked.

The officers looked at each other and laughed. "Y ahora un soborno? Usted va al carcel, también!" one said.

"No, senores, no estoy tratando de sobornar a ustedes, estoy solamente ofreciendo a pagar sus multas. Despues de esto, ellos van a regresar a su país."

"One-hundred dollars," the reply came in perfect English.

"I don't have that much. How much money do you guys have?" Chad asked us.

I had $80 or $90 in my back pocket in case my wallet was stolen. "I've got $30," I said, pulling my wallet from my front pocket and counting the bills.

"I've got $22," Brad said as he counted a folded wad of money he removed from his front pocket.

Chad counted $23 in his wallet, saying, "That's exactly $75." He took the cash and repeated to the officers, "Solamente tenemos 75 pesos. Cogelo todo--para las multas." He stressed the latter part and added, "De acuerdo. Vamos."

One officer took the money, folded it, and slipped it inside his shirt pocket, and said, "Estúpidos gringos. Regresen a mami y a papi." They laughed, turned, and left.

We weren't in a mood to celebrate our good fortune. We determined that we had enough of Tijuana and returned to Chad's car. Luckily it was where we parked it.

We thanked Chad for saving our asses. "It's no telling what would have happened if you hadn't seen them taking us," I said to Chad as we slowly drove North toward the border in his sputtering automobile, which I feared would break down, stranding us in that God-forsaken country.

"They wanted money. They would have taken what you had and let you go," Chad said. "They don't have time to mess with you. They'll pull that trick on ten more desperate Americans caught in the wrong place at the right time tonight."

"They probably set us up," Brad offered.

"Wouldn't doubt it," Chad responded. "Just another way of ripping off gringos."

"I didn't know you knew Spanish," I said from the rear seat, slapping Chad on the back.

"You never asked!" came his sarcastic reply.

My heart raced as we waited in one of the several long lines of cars at the border. Every possible fear crossed my mind, and I worried we weren't free from the grasp of Mexican authorities.

"What if they called ahead to be on the lookout for us?" I asked.

"For pissing in an alley?" Chad laughed. "The Border Patrol wants to catch drug runners."

We reached a U.S. Border Patrol officer. "Citizenship?" he requested, leaning on the Chad's door, and looking into the car. I watched his eyes search the interior as well as we three occupants.

"USA," Chad calmly replied.

"All of you?"

"Yes, sir."

There was a pause. My pulse raced, and my palms became damp. Maybe I was having a panic attack.

"Purpose of your visit to Mexico?"

"Sightseeing," Chad responded. "These two are tourists from Tennessee."

"Anything to report?"

"No, sir."

I started to mention my painting but realized that in the excitement of our detainment and release, I left it at the El Cid. I didn't have one Mexican souvenir, except a pounding tequila headache and a memory that would be greatly exaggerated with time.

"Please pull over to the side behind that blue car," the officer pointed toward a Camaro.

"Crap," Chad gasped and followed directions. "I was afraid of this."

"What do they want?" I inquired with obvious worry.

"They'll search the car for drugs," Chad responded.

"There's nothing to worry about, is there?" Brad asked.

"We're cool," Chad said. "I know better than have shit in the car going to and coming from Mexico. I took out my stash and left it at home."

"What the fuck are you talking about?" Brad asked.

"You had drugs in here?" I shouted.

"Keep it down. I told you we're cool. Nothing to worry about, Chad replied.

"Jesus!" I sighed.

An officer politely asked us to exit the vehicle. He examined each of us with his eyes but didn't search us. He used a flashlight to inspect every crevice in the car. He opened the front-end trunk, which was filled with beach supplies. He opened the rear engine compartment and performed a quick inspection. The car's interior was given a thorough search.

We watched the officer perform his duty with meticulous precision. I was scared shitless that he might find drugs. Chad was true to his word and had nothing illegal in his car. I prayed he was truthful.

The officer concluded his business and said, "Thanks for your patience. Have a nice evening, boys."

We entered the car and resumed our journey home.

"I almost shit my pants," Brad said.

Chad laughed and replied, "I told you not to worry. I always have things under control."

I heaved a huge sigh of relief, entered the rear seat, and

leaned my head back, falling fast asleep until we reached Janie's driveway and the satisfaction of arriving safely.

Our adventure remained a secret from Janie and Chuck. We didn't need to hear "I told you so." Brad and I were building a treasury of secrets and would be indebted to each other for life.

Two days before our departure, Chad invited us to a going away party at Balboa Park with our new friends. It was the wildest night of my life. The park was packed with hippies in tie-dyed clothing. People were dancing, blowing bubbles, selling trinkets, reading aloud, and carrying signs protesting the war and promoting various causes. Vanilla Fudge's version of The Supremes' *You Keep Me Hangin' On* blared from a radio. I heard a couple discussing the controversial movie, *Rosemary's Baby*. There was an art show in one corner of the park, featuring mainly psychedelic paintings. Marijuana odor infiltrated the air.

We joined our friends and were offered our choice of an Olympia beer, a joint that was being passed, or both. Someone mentioned that some good mescaline was available. I accepted a beer. As the evening grew late, the party grew louder and rowdy. Chad approached me with a thin girl with long, braided blonde hair, graced with a string of fresh daisies, grasping his arm with both her hands.

"Carly, this is Steve. Steve, this is Carly," he said, smiled, and left.

"Bradley said you're from Tennessee," she said, flashing a wide smile, dominated by strong, perfect teeth. The only person who called him Bradley was his mother and only when she was angry.

"Yeah," I responded, stunned by her beauty.

She sat and continued, "Tell me everything about it.

I've never been there."

After a lengthy discussion and several beers (she also smoked grass), we began kissing. I normally wouldn't have made out in public, but the alcohol made it easier. It was love at first sight.

Carly gently took my hand and stood. "Come with me," she said. "I have a car."

I walked with her to a 1959 four-door, two-tone green Pontiac Star Chief that had peace signs painted on the doors, hood, and trunk. She opened a rear door, entered, and pulled me in after her. She immediately attacked me with kisses and fondling. For the second time in my young life, I had sex in a car. What a wonderful way to end this unbelievable vacation.

Carly left. I wrote her twice after returning to Knoxville, but she never responded. I often wonder what happened to her.

I walked back to join Brad. I questioned why he set me up with Carly instead of keeping her for himself. I hoped they hadn't had sex, too.

As I neared the campfire, I saw a guy with long, stringy blonde hair kick dirt at Brad, which interrupted him kissing a girl.

"What the fuck, dude," the guy shouted and kicked more dirt. "She's my chick."

Brad rose and said, "Sorry man. I didn't know."

The guy pushed Brad, causing him to fall. I realized that he was going to kick Brad, and I quickly joined the scene and pushed the guy, knocking him down. He jumped to his feet and took an awkward swing at me, but I dodged. I believe he was high on something. Brad was on his feet and ready to fight once the guy regained his feet.

"Johnny, it didn't mean anything. We were just being friendly," the girl said. "Please leave him alone."

"Stop the shit," came a loud command. The voice belonged to Chad. He stood between the three of us. "I can't believe my friends are fighting on such a peaceful night. Is this the way you want to end your California trip?" He turned toward Brad and me.

"What's the problem?" Chad asked.

"This dude was making out with Cheryl," the guy replied.

"I didn't know she is his girl," Brad defended himself.

"Let's all relax and enjoy what's left of the night. Have a beer," Chad smiled, aware he had diffused the situation.

We sat around the fire and opened beers. "Thanks for protecting me," Brad laughed and hit his can against mine.

"It's about time it's the other way around," I replied.

Janie, Chuck, and the boys took Brad and me to Anza Borriego State Park, followed by dinner, and to see the movie, *Winning,* with Paul Newman, our last day. It was a busy, yet quiet and appropriate ending to what I recall as one of the best times of my life.

I learned my lesson from my first flight to Washington and bought Dramamine and swallowed two pills to ease my stomach for the long return flight. I believe our airline was Frontier, but I am not positive. I slept most of the way until we reached a layover and changed planes in Denver. I was thrilled when the plane taxied at Knoxville's McGee-Tyson Airport, delivering us safely to Tennessee.

The California trip passed quickly. Only the Tijuana incident marred an otherwise perfect vacation, and that became an instant bragging rite for us. I began a journal after returning because I didn't want to forget anything about that memorable Summer. It helps me recall the amorous adventures of two carefree teenagers who often were foolish, yet typified youths in that alleged age of innocence.

I learned much and matured in a short period. I changed politically from conservative to somewhat liberal. Just as with the previous Summer, I recognized it would be difficult to return to restrictive parents after the freedom we gained in California. My parents would be upset with Janie and Chuck if they knew how much liberty we were allowed. Many decisions awaited me in the coming year that concerned the draft, college, and my future. Skip's death continued to haunt me, and if I drew a low number in the lottery, I pondered if I truly would flee to Canada.

I wonder what happened to Chad.

Summer ended on a high note. Far away in Bethel Rock, New York, The Woodstock Festival took the country by storm August 15 to18. Billed as *An Aquarian Exposition: 3 Days of Peace and Music*, it entered the annals of music history. I was too young to consider attending, but as I grew older, I dreamt of how amazing it would be to have been there. Brad and I shared several adventures, and more awaited us; however, I can't imagine what we would have experienced had we been at Woodstock. I could fill volumes about the craziness we might have encountered for three days. In hindsight, I am thankful we weren't there. The album, *Woodstock*, with music from the original soundtrack and movie, was my favorite record my freshman year in college.

16

"S-S, S-E-N. I-I, I-O-R. S-E-N-I-O-R! Senior!" we screamed the chant at the top of our lungs at the opening assembly of our last year at Claremont High. We finally made it!

Brad and I returned to our normal routines upon our return from California. We told our friends about our unbelievable trip West, and they eventually pleaded with us to please stop talking about it. Brad played football, and I busied myself with Royals activities, unaware that I was less than a month from resigning. I designed a recruitment program that hopefully would attract prospects away from the Kings and Juniors and improve the Royals' image. Many sophomores chose to decline social club membership because of the rumors, mostly factual, they heard about hell week and initiation. If the Royals abandoned the brutal rite of passage and the other two clubs maintained the practice, I believed we would entice more of their recruits to lean our way. Unfortunately, it was not to be.

I enjoyed high school and wanted to make the most of my last year. The previous Spring, I ran for parliamentarian of Student Council and lost. I was disappointed, but the incoming president appointed me chair of the Social and Activities Committee, considered the most prestigious committee. Our responsibilities included planning the Fall TWIRP (The Woman is Required to Pay) Dance and the Spring Carnival. For the TWIRP Dance, the girls invited the boys. The theme of our dance was Li'l Abner, and attendees dressed like characters in the comic strip. My co-chair was Jennifer Jones, and since neither of us was dating anyone, we went together and thoroughly enjoyed the evening we created. Many students and teachers expressed to Jennifer and me that the activities we planned that year were the best they'd seen at Claremont.

....

I was studying after supper in my room when the door opened, and Brad barged in. I almost lost my temper because I assumed it was one of my parents entering without knocking.

"Hey, fart face," he said. "What 'cha doing, playing with yourself?"

"Do you normally walk in someone's room without knocking? What if I was? You'd be upset."

"No, I believe you would be upset."

"What are you doing here instead of calling? If I know you, you want something. How was practice?"

"Short. Just drills. No pads. Home opener tomorrow night. Are you going?"

"Yeah, the Royals are going to the game and to the Armory afterward. The Soul Sanction is playing. They're the band that won the Jaycee State Battle of the Bands. They're amazing. I love their horn section."

I waited for his reason for barging into my room uninvited.

"You're not going to believe the plan I have for us," he said, sitting on the edge of my bed.

"Oh, no, do I want to hear this? Every time you have a bright idea, it costs me something and results in trouble, and I get grounded."

"No, I'm serious about this. I've been thinking since we returned from California that I owe you big time for inviting me on that trip. It was the best time of my life." He paused.

"Go on. I'm all ears," I laughed.

"I want you to be on my ticket for president and vice president of the senior class. Of course, I'll head the ticket and you will be my vice president."

I was caught off-guard. "Are you fucking serious? What have you been smoking?"

"I've given this a lot of thought ever since I saw the announcement for candidates in the daily bulletin. I don't want to ask anyone else, and you and I do everything well together. We're a good team. We'll have a blast, and it will look good on our college applications."

I realized he was serious but repeated, "You're really serious? If not, it's a sick joke."

"I swear to God. I've never been so serious in my life."

"Let me think about it," I stalled.

"What's there to think about? The application deadline is Monday."

"Who else is running?"

"How the hell do I know? They said they'll announce the candidates on Tuesday morning."

My excitement mounting, I quickly agreed. "What do we do next?"

"After you sign the application, I'll submit it tomorrow. You remember the senior class election last year? We do what they did. We create a theme, write a skit, and follow the rules. Let's get together this weekend and develop a plan."

He stood and slapped my back. "I have to get home. We have an 8:00 curfew on nights before games, and if I'm not home when one of the coaches call, they'll bench me first quarter of the game."

"I'll work on some ideas. We need a good campaign manager," I offered, but he had already disappeared from the room.

It was hard to concentrate on homework because ideas about the class election flooded my brain. I was amazed that

Brad wanted to do this. He usually avoided the spotlight. The weekend couldn't arrive soon enough for me.

Brad and I met briefly at lunch, and I signed the application. I went to the game that night with the Royals and to the dance afterward. The football team lost to the West Rebels, and the players arrived late to the dance. I didn't bother Brad because I presumed that he was in a bad mood following the loss. I was aware that if I left the Royals to hang with Brad and his football buddies and Kings brothers, the Royals would give me a hard time about deserting them *for the enemy*, the same accusation leveled at me during hell week.

The Social and Activities Committee and the Key Club were assigned clean-up of the stadium on Saturday morning. Attendance was good from both groups, and we finished early and played a football game afterward on the field. Key Club was one of the more prestigious organizations at school, and I became friends with the president, Terry Dorsey, through Student Council. They honored me with a bid to join a month later, and I gladly accepted because it filled the void left after I resigned from the Royals.

After lunch, I called Brad and asked if he wanted to come over and discuss the election. He agreed but didn't want to talk about the football game. He said that he played horribly, and the coaches were pissed with the team's performance. The loss hurt Claremont in the District standings.

I had a note tablet ready to take notes when Brad joined me in my room.

"What should we decide first?" I asked.

"The campaign manager," he replied.

"Let's list possibilities."

"We shouldn't pick an athlete. Some students don't like athletes, and we need someone everyone knows and will appeal to the most seniors."

I agreed, and we paused to consider names.

"By the way, Brad," I continued, "why did you pick me?"

"I told you. I want to thank you for the California trip."

"That's it?"

"Hey, man, you're my best friend, and we need to go out on top. It's our senior year."

I was surprised. He had never called me his best friend. Even if we lost the election, his admission was enough of a win for me.

"Thanks. That means a lot," I paused. "I believe we should get a girl. With two guys running, we need to appeal to the senior girls. They're already attracted to you, but I don't want to take chances."

"Good point," he said. "Do you have the junior yearbook?" The senior yearbook wouldn't be published until Spring.

"Yep," I replied, taking the yearbook from my shelf.

We thumbed through the junior pictures, noting names of potential girls for our campaign manager. We compiled a list of seven names and discussed the pros and cons of each.

We narrowed it to two, Nancy Anderson and Melissa Vanderburg. Nancy was a cheerleader and member of a social club. Melissa served as president of the junior class and was also in a social club.

"Hard choice," I said.

Brad nodded and said, "Let's go with Melissa if she doesn't run against us. She has the experience from last year and is liked by everyone."

"Sounds good to me."

"Melissa will make a good campaign manager."

"And if she's running, should we go with Nancy?"

"Probably, but if Melissa runs, I'll try to learn who she

asked to be her campaign manager. That might make a difference. Nancy and Melissa are friends, and Nancy may not want to campaign against her."

"That's settled," I continued. "What's next?"

Brad searched his memory and replied, "They'll announce the candidates on Tuesday morning and meet with us afterward to provide the rules and guidelines for the election. Our campaign committee will spend the rest of the week hanging signs and distributing flyers to seniors and asking for their vote."

"What about the skit?" I asked.

"Yeah, I forgot about that. The skits and speeches are next Wednesday. You're a good writer. Are you willing to find someone to help you write the skit? You can write a draft and run it by the campaign committee for additional ideas and approval. I'll help as much as I can."

Besides hanging flyers and banners, each presidential candidate prepared a ten-minute skit that was presented in the school auditorium prior to the presidential candidate's campaign speech.

"Who do we want on the campaign committee?" I asked.

"We can have as many as we want. Once we get our manager, we'll have a meeting and develop plans for the campaign. We can meet in a classroom because we don't have enough room at your house or mine. Start asking your friends to help. Get the senior Key Clubbers behind you. Depending on who runs, I should have the senior athletes wrapped up. The senior Kings won't be an issue."

"I hope Melissa doesn't run," I added. "If she runs, we'll split votes."

Brad agreed and thumbed through the junior pictures in the yearbook again. "We need to work on my speech," he noted.

Luckily, only the presidential candidates speak at the assembly. I was relieved I didn't have to speak for the vice president position. "When is voting?"

"The senior assembly is next week on Wednesday, and after that, they'll vote in the auditorium lobby," Brad responded. "They'll announce the winners for the junior and senior elections over the PA before the dismissal bell that afternoon."

We spent another hour discussing preliminary plans and noting names for the campaign committee. Everyone involved didn't have to be a senior, and a few sophomore and junior names were added to the list. We remembered that a talented artist was required to design posters and flyers, and we agreed to ask Ryan Bailey, a junior. The school supplied the campaign materials to allow everyone an equal opportunity; otherwise, candidates with access to a money supply would have an unfair advantage.

"That's enough for today," Brad said, placing the yearbook on my desk. "I'll catch you later." He gave me a thumbs up and left for home.

"Start working on your speech," I called after him.

My excitement increased about the pending campaign and election. How awesome would it be if we won?

We attended the rules meeting on Monday, where we learned that our opponents were Betsy Day, president, and Lisa Somerfield, vice president. Betsy was a majorette, member of the tennis team, and social club member. Lisa was involved in various activities and in the same social club as Betsy. Both were well known with the senior class but being in the same club would hurt them in gaining votes from the other girls' clubs members.

Brad and I left the meeting and continued our

discussion at lunch. "How's it look?" I asked. "What do you believe our chances are against Betsy and Lisa?"

"Really good," he replied. "I'll ask Melissa to head our campaign, and she'll pull in a ton of votes for us. We've got this in the bag."

"I wouldn't go that far," I warned. "I've learned never assume anything. Let's work our asses off and earn this thing."

"You're right, as usual. I need you to take the lead with Melissa on the activities this week. With football practice and meetings, I am booked. Can you go to the office and reserve a classroom for a meeting after school? We can spread the word to as many folks as possible to attend the organizational meeting. Since there isn't much notice, attendance will be light. In fact, reserve the room for every day up to next Wednesday. If someone offers their house, we can switch locations. We can start after football practice every day but today. I should be able to attend the remainder of the meetings."

"Sounds like a plan," I replied. "Let me know what Melissa says."

The week flew past. The campaign meetings went well. We had more volunteers than we needed, which proved to be an asset. Everyone had a task. Every area where posters and flyers were allowed were filled with our material. Someone hung a sign on the back of a stall in the boy's restroom that read, "Dump on Brad". We had a good laugh and assumed it was placed there by a Juniors club member.

I asked Melissa if she would help write the skit, and she was thrilled to assist. We brainstormed ideas and concluded we wanted a skit that contained elements that surprised the audience because it wasn't like anything that had previously been done. Two committee members, brother and sister, were gifted singers and played guitars. We met with them and asked them to perform an original song written for the skit. They agreed, and we four wrote a short song to the tune of the song, *Frankie and Johnny*. I don't remember the entire lyrics except the opening:

> *This is the start of our story.*
> *About a young man and his fame.*
> *They called him Funky Chicken,*
> *but Brad Erickson was his real name.*
> *He is our man*
> *For president.*

The skit featured a superhero character, Funky Chicken, who eliminated crime and bad scenarios we created on stage. Funky Chicken, played by a skinny male committee member, was supposed to be Brad in disguise. At one point in the skit, we rigged a climbing rope we borrowed from the gym, and Funky Chicken flew onto stage like Tarzan and stopped two muggers from assaulting a girl student.

The main surprise element was that we learned that at the rear of the stage, there was a cargo door large enough for a car to drive onto stage. I didn't know it existed. One of the Kings drove a Volkswagen Beetle which we borrowed for the skit. We pushed it behind the rear curtain without starting the engine and informing the audience that a car was on stage. A scene in the skit approached when the curtain was pulled back and several guys pushed the car into view. The curtain was left slightly open at the driver's door side, and twenty members of the skit came through the curtain, through the front seat, and out the passenger door. It was a hilarious scene, and the audience cheered. It appeared as though all the individuals had been in the car. Several people later asked me how we got the car on stage. The scene was reminiscent of the skit at the

Summer playground circus many years earlier when we pulled the same stunt with the Keystone Cops and their car.

The next scene featured the two singers in front of the closed curtain. The song reviewed what the audience witnessed in the skit, and when they came to the verse,

> *They called him Funky Chicken,*
> *but Brad Erickson was his real name*,

Brad came through the curtain with a shy shrug, huge smile, and waved to the audience, which loudly cheered his appearance.

The night before the assembly, we practiced the skit and ran through the checklist of everything to do. There was nothing more to do. I cornered Brad as we left the classroom and inquired about his speech.

"Did you finish your speech?"

"Almost."

"Don't wait to the last minute. Do you mind if I read it? Maybe I can give you some pointers and suggest items you may not have included."

He opened a notebook and handed several sheets of hand-written notes to me. "Bring it over tonight so I can review it. It's already late, and by the time I get home and have supper, it will be much later."

"No problem. I'll work on it first thing after I eat."

I edited the speech with Indy 500 speed following supper. I repeated a dozen times to my parents why I was eating fast. Brad's draft was better than I expected. I added a few points and corrected grammar. I typed the speech on my old Royal typewriter for him because he would find it easier to read a typed copy versus a hand-written version. After giving him the speech and wishing him good luck at his front door, I returned home for a restless night's sleep.

By coin flip, Betsy Day's skit and speech were first. Both were well received with applause and cheers from the audience of seniors. There was a ten-minute break while we replaced Betsy and Lisa's props with ours on stage. I hoped our skit would blow Betsy's out of the water.

The senior class faculty advisor thanked Betsy and Lisa and introduced Brad and me for our skit and Brad's speech.

Once the two singers finished and Brad made his appearance through the curtain, he went to the podium, made an audible sigh, and began,

"Fellow seniors. I am Brad Erickson, and I am running for your class president. My running mate for class vice president is Steve Jackson.

"We are honored to stand before you today, as are our opponents. Steve and I have known each other since the sixth grade, and we are as close as brothers." I wasn't aware that Brad had added that sentence, and I glanced at him with appreciation.

"I tell you that because it is important for you to know how well we work together. Many of you may believe that president and vice president are merely symbolic offices. But I ask you symbolic of what? We don't plan to sit idly and wait for graduation next June where we will represent you at Commencement. We want to spend the next nine months representing you to the administration and being active in the major activities at school.

"Along with our superb campaign manager, Melissa Vanderburg, who did an excellent job as junior class president," (There were cheers for Melissa and a shout, 'Go Melissa!') "and our hard-working campaign committee, we have discussed various plans and projects that will set a precedent for future senior class officers.

"For starters, we want to raise money and become the first class ever to leave a class gift to Claremont High School. We want every senior involved in this goal so that each of you can look back in future years and remember what your class left for your alma mater.

"Sometimes promises are not fulfilled, but Steve and I promise to have the best senior prom in school history!" There were cheers and applause. "It's all about the venue and the band, and we will strive to improve on both. We want you to always remember your senior prom.

"Today you will also vote for class treasurer and secretary, and regardless of who is elected, we will bring them on board with our team and work closely with them to achieve our goals. I said 'our goals' because we share them with you.

"We want to hear from you starting with our first day in office through the remainder of our term in office. We will hold monthly town halls to give updates and solicit input and suggestions from you. We will also provide a means for you to submit suggestions, comments, complaints, or whatever anonymously.

"Both Steve and I have a good working relationship with the administration. That is important. I believe that most of you know me and are aware that I have dedicated three years to junior varsity and varsity athletics. I am dedicated to academics and maintain a B average.

You may ask why am I running for class president and why Steve is running for vice president? The answer is simple. Because we care. High school has been the best years of our lives. I will always remember the good times, and yes, some bad ones, at Claremont High. I haven't graduated, and I already look forward to future class reunions." There were audible laughs in the audience. Someone yelled, "We'll miss you, Brad!" More laughter. Brad smiled and responded, "I'll miss you, too!" More laughter.

"Most of you also know Steve," Brad continued. "He has been as involved in co-curricular activities as I have been in athletics. We know this school. We are proud to be seniors and proud to be Knights!

"In conclusion, Steve and I will be honored to serve as your president and vice president, and we ask that you support us with your vote. Thank you, and let's go Knights!"

I came from side stage and joined Brad with raised clasped hands, with smiles bigger than Texas. There was loud applause, and many of our fellow students, particularly Brad's teammates and club brothers and the senior Royals, were standing. Many shouted, "Brad! Brad! Brad!" Others chanted, "Let's go Knights! Let's go Knights!" The Knight was our mascot.

It was a moment I'll never forget, undoubtedly the highlight of my senior year.

After casting our vote in the lobby, Brad and I went to class. The day dragged at a snail's pace. I couldn't concentrate in my classes and ate little of my lunch. Classmates continuously wished me good luck.

I had English last period. I have no idea what the topic was that day because I watched the minutes crawl by on the classroom clock. Athletes had physical education the last class period so that they could begin practice early for their respective sports. The Tennessee Secondary School Athletic Association limited daily practice time, but the coaches utilized the last period, which didn't count toward practice time.

The ding of the PA system finally sounded. The classroom became hauntingly quiet. I felt the stares darting from my classmates. Betsy had friends and club sisters in my class, so there wasn't unanimous support for Brad and me.

"Students, attention please," I recognized the principal's voice. "I want to announce the results of the junior and senior class elections. First, the junior class officers for 1969-70 are…." Jesus, I had to wait through the junior class winners. My stomach was in knots.

"And the 1969-70 senior class officers are…." He announced the treasurer and secretary winners. There were a few cheers in the class and then quiet. "Serving as president and vice president of the senior class are," he paused. "Brad Erickson and Steve Jackson!"

"Holy shit!" I cried. The class erupted in applause and cheers, and several classmates slapped my back and extended congratulations. I was in a haze. I was optimistic yet prepared to be humiliated by a loss. My teacher shouted, "Congratulations, Steve!"

The bell sounded, and I ran to the gymnasium, not stopping at my locker, but I was delayed by students along the way who congratulated me. Brad assumed that I would come and waited outside the locker room. We shared a hug and huge smiles.

"We fucking won!" he exclaimed. "Can you believe it?"

"It hasn't sunk in," I replied.

"We'll celebrate tonight. We're lucky there's no game. Get in touch with everyone and decide where to go. I'll check in with you when I get home. Remind me to call Betsy and thank her for a good campaign."

"Erickson, let's go!" a coach screamed.

"Later, Steve. I don't want to run extra laps," he called, running through the door toward the practice field.

During our senior year, we completed the campaign promises. We held a superb senior prom at the new Hyatt Regency adjacent to the Civic Coliseum. Concern about the driving distance to the hotel was expressed by some parents because they feared students would drink and drive. The administration helped alleviate the fear by warning students that their graduation could be affected if there was an incident involving alcohol.

We held car washes, cleaned the stadium following the remaining home football games, hosted bake sales, and sponsored several other projects to raise money for the class gift. Several parents donated to our effort, which raised $5,000. We discussed several gift options at our Senior Class Steering Committee meetings and settled on a bronze sculpture of a knight. It would bear a plaque noting it as a gift of the class of 1970. The committee members discussed several locations for the sculpture but couldn't agree on a final site. We left that decision to the administration, who placed it in a glass case in the school lobby after its delivery the following Spring.

We hosted two town halls that Fall to receive feedback and suggestions from those in attendance. One recommendation was to allow seniors a "Bermuda Shorts Day" when they could wear shorts to school. We approached the principal with the idea, and it was approved. The second request was to allow seniors to leave campus for lunch, but that was soundly rejected. Safety and a time factor were cited as reasons.

Due to Brad's heavy athletic schedule, he had little involvement with the Senior Class Steering Committee. I took the lead and ultimately became de facto president. I didn't mind because I enjoyed the opportunity and attention that came with the responsibility. Brad's final duty as class president came in June when he provided remarks at our graduation ceremony. I was proud that all four of the class officers were seated on stage with the principal, the superintendent, and a United States congressman.

17

The Monday after Thanksgiving is another of those days I'll never forget. I arrived at the school lobby and was greeted by an atmosphere of quiet and gloom. The normally loud chatter was missing. Students were hugging, and a few were silently crying.

"What's going on?" I asked Stacy Keen, a friend. "Did something happen?"

"Oh, Steve, it's so sad," she replied. "Billy Baker killed himself."

The shock hit, but my memory went blank. Who was Billy Baker? I tried to paint a face with no luck. "Who's Billy?" I asked.

"You know him. He was a sophomore. He played in that band with David Williams."

I recognized David and pictured members of the band and remembered Billy as the bass player. "I remember him. Long hair. Stayed pretty much to himself."

"That's him," Stacy replied, tears flowing down her cheeks. We embraced, her head on my shoulder.

"That's horrible," I said. "Do they know why?"

"No. It's so sad. He was quiet, but he was a nice guy."

The morning bell sounded, giving us five minutes to report to first period. My class was biology. I walked into class, which also served as a laboratory. The room reeked of formaldehyde. There was quiet talk but not the normal loud chatter. The PA sounded for the morning announcements.

The principal cleared his throat and began, "Students," he said and paused. "As some of you may know, and for others, I am sorry to report that one of our sophomore students, Billy Baker, passed away over the weekend. This is a sad day for Claremont High, and we are aware that this will have a negative impact on many of you. The district office provided extra counselors to assist our counseling staff in meeting with those of you who may want to share your feelings with someone. We highly encourage you to do so. Your teachers will provide a pass for anyone who wants to meet with a counselor.

"We will hold a memorial program for Billy and will provide information once it is scheduled. Again, I ask you to speak to someone, not only about Billy, but if you are struggling with anything that is affecting you personally or academically. We are here for you. We will dispense with further announcements until tomorrow."

We sat in stunned silence. Memories of Skip's death resurfaced, and now I had to deal with the loss of a fellow student. I couldn't stop asking why? What was so bad in his life that he didn't want to live? We will never know the answer. I wondered how he did it. Did he leave a note? I felt sorry for his parents. Did he have brothers and sisters? I couldn't get my mind off Billy, and I didn't know him. My teacher was speaking, but I missed the words. I wanted the day to end.

Dinner was unbearable that evening. The atmosphere was as cloudy as a cold, Winter day. The competition was intense on who would speak first. I was content with the silence. My food was tasteless. Mom spoke, "Steve, if there ever is a time you need to talk, talk about anything, I hope you know we are here for you."

I nodded and remained silent.

My parents gave each other a quick, questioning glance.

"Did you know this boy?" Dad asked.

"Not personally, but I know who he was. He played in a garage band with some other kids I know," I responded emotionless. I concluded that I was unusually upset about Billy because I still grieved for Skip.

Even though I didn't know Billy well, I felt the need to attend his funeral. I never learned how he died, although the rumor mill ran rampant. Most friends with whom I spoke believed he shot himself.

The funeral was attended by many family members and friends. It was a school day, and students who attended were given an excused absence. I didn't want to go alone or with my mother, and I convinced Stacy to attend since she informed me about his death. It was an extremely depressing service, and I had constant flashbacks from Skip's funeral. Stacy and I walked by the open casket prior to the service, and I froze. I couldn't continue past the casket. I glanced at Billy, and suddenly tears streamed down my face. I couldn't stop weeping. Stacy took my hand and told me it's okay. I wiped the tears with my coat sleeve and responded that I was fine. I crossed myself and joined other friends in a pew.

"I don't know what came over me," I whispered embarrassingly to Stacy.

"It's ok. Don't worry. It's hard to accept losing a young friend," she replied.

I shook my head, still questioning my reaction.

Following the service, we decided to not go to the cemetery for the burial. I took Stacy home and returned to my house, glad that Dad was at work and Mom was shopping. I needed to be alone to clear my head and move past the depressing day. I took Bob Dylan's *The Times They are a-Changin'* album off the shelf and played the title track. How appropriate for a teenager facing challenges and changing times in the turbulent sixties.

Teenagers are resilient, and a week later, routines were back to normal. Three weeks remained until Christmas break. Since resigning from the Royals, Key Club consumed my spare time. We completed various school projects and raised money that was applied toward a scholarship for a graduating senior. I was honored to receive the scholarship the following Spring.

My favorite Key Club project was visiting East Tennessee Psychiatric Hospital, which was located a few miles from our neighborhood. On Sunday afternoons, Key Club members visited a boy's wing at the hospital and played games and participated in other activities with the residents.

When I first learned about the weekly visit to the hospital, I was hesitant to attend. I questioned the mental state of the children. Was it safe? What were the conditions at the hospital? Were the children ever violent? I promised Terry Dorcey I would attend if he stayed with me until I was comfortable with the surroundings. I was nervous but quickly adjusted to the environment and enjoyed playing with the children. The boys' favorite activity was playing football, although our games didn't resemble the sport because of their physical and mental disabilities. The visits were often challenging and frustrating, but I looked forward to them because I grew attached to the kids, mainly from sympathy. They were starved for attention and outside companionship. Each visit reminded me of the blessings I had in my life and that I should be more thankful for them. I remembered to mention the kids in my prayers at mass.

Because of my anticipation for the Sunday visits, I invited Brad to tag along on our next trip, even though he wasn't a Key Club member. His versatile personality fit perfectly with the environment, and I believed he would be enthralled with the situation and enjoy the encounter with the young residents.

His initial reaction was the same as my first gut feeling. "Are you kidding me?" he exclaimed. "You want me to go with you and play football with a bunch of crazy kids?"

"They're not crazy," I responded. "Some have physical disabilities, and others have mental issues. If I didn't believe you'd enjoy it, I wouldn't ask. There's one kid, his name is Ricky, probably about 12 or 13, and he can throw the football good. We're there less than two hours, and there's staff supervision. Come on, you big chicken, how about it?"

Maybe calling him chicken provided the impetus for him to give the invitation serious consideration.

"Are you sure it's safe?"

"Seriously, Brad, you're acting like I normally act, not you. Don't be a wimp. What do you usually do on Sundays? It's after mass, so you can't use that as an excuse."

"Okay, I'll go, but if anything happens, I'll never let you live it down."

Brad became visibly anxious as our two cars of seven guys stopped at the guard gate at the hospital's entrance. I was surprised at how much freedom we had once we entered the grounds. There were a series of buildings that lined the roads. The landscaping was simple. Oak trees abounded and the grass was well manicured. It felt more like a small college campus than a mental hospital. We parked in the lot at the wing where our kids were housed. We entered and were immediately mobbed by the young boys. They were glad to see us, probably the only contact with the outside world for most if not all of them. "Hey, St…St…Steve," Ricky jogged to me and shook my hand. I was happy that I had impressed him enough for him to remember my name.

"This is Brad, Ricky," I said. "Brad is a star player on our high school football team."

"Not really," Brad said, blushing and shaking Ricky's hand.

"What po-po-si-si-tion do you pl-pl-ay?" Ricky

stuttered.

"Tailback," Brad responded, showing comfort with the new situation. His anxiety was diminished by the friendliness of the kids.

"Ca-ca-can we play foot-foot-ball?" Ricky asked.

"Let me check with the supervisor and ask if it's okay," I responded.

Once we were cleared to take the boys outside, a staff member and we walked across the road to a large grassy field and divided into two teams, although some of the boys switched back and forth between teams. It was impossible to coordinate a true game, and we faked the rules and played the best we could. No one was offsides or called for penalties. I don't remember that anyone caught a pass, which frustrated Ricky. Each of the kids wanted to play quarterback, and it was difficult convincing them to take turns.

As predicted, Brad befriended Ricky and practiced throwing with him. Much patience was needed to survive the afternoon, but it was fun and worth the effort. The smiles on the kids' faces worked wonders for our morale. We grew tired of playing football and returned the kids inside where a small snack was waiting. Several of the boys were too shy to go outside and remained in the multi-purpose room. We attempted contact with them but learned that they preferred to be left alone. The more outgoing kids peppered us with questions and remained at our side. Some were too touchy, and we gently pushed their hands away. When the two hours expired, we were ready to depart. I was impressed with the staff that worked with the kids eight hours a day. I didn't have the patience for that kind of work.

Brad talked about the day's adventure on the entire ride home.

"What do you believe is wrong with Ricky?" he asked.

"He seems normal to me, except for the stutter."

"No idea," I said. "Maybe he's low on the retardation scale."

"Nice kid," Brad added. "I feel sorry for him—for all of them. We don't realize how fortunate we are until experiencing something like today. I'm glad you talked me into going. I hope I can go back."

"Yeah, you big chicken," I laughed.

"Screw you!" Brad punched my arm.

"Watch out, dirt bag. I'm driving!"

18

My parents purchased a new car for an early Christmas present to themselves, and as a surprise, they gave their old car, the one I wrecked, to me. I was thrilled! The last six months of my senior year and I had access to my own car. I couldn't wait to call Brad.

"No shit?" he shouted. "That's great! You need to get another girlfriend so we can double."

"What do you mean, I need to get a girlfriend? What about you?"

"I've been seeing Melanie Underwood occasionally."

"I know. I've seen you in the hallways. Looks serious to me," I joked.

"No way. I'm not ready to settle down."

"She's got you wrapped around her little finger. Yes, dear. Whatever you say, dear. Yes, dear," I mocked in a soprano voice.

"Go to hell. I gotta go. Catch you later, asshole," he hung up, not waiting for a reply.

I laughed, went to my room, and plopped down on my bed. My radio blasted Steam's *Na Na Hey Hey Kiss Him Goodbye*, a song Claremont students adopted and sang to visitors at home basketball games when we won. I was happy.

Randy Thomas was one of Brad's Kings brothers. His sister attended Tennessee Tech University in Cookeville. Her boyfriend's fraternity was hosting a Homecoming party, and she invited Randy for the weekend. He didn't want to go alone and asked Brad, and Brad inquired if I could go. I believe Brad had accepted the idea that when he and I were together, a good time was had and something crazy was likely to occur. I convinced my parents to allow me to join my friends because it was an opportunity to tour the university, and I was in the process of applying to colleges and universities.

We drove to Cookeville Saturday morning and stayed at Randy's sister's apartment. I was excited to experience college life because I would enter college in less than a year. That night we attended the Homecoming concert with Smokey Robinson and the Miracles. I was a huge Motown fan, and their song, *Baby, Baby Don't* Cry, was one of my favorites. Our seats were at the top of the facility in obstructed view, but we didn't mind because we saw Smokey Robinson in person.

The fraternity party followed the concert at a rental hall near campus. We worried that the fraternity may not allow three high school kids to attend, but Randy's sister convinced us it wasn't a problem. She said they would assume we were freshmen.

We heard the music blaring once we pulled into the parking lot. We entered the hall with Randy's sister and her boyfriend and immediately were confronted with the strong odor of beer and cigarette smoke.

"Okay, guys, you're on your own," Randy's sister said. "Have fun and be careful. Stay out of trouble."

We soaked in the atmosphere of our first fraternity party. I was curious because I wasn't familiar with fraternities and assumed I might be recruited to join at whatever university I chose to attend. I didn't have an interest in joining a fraternity because I compared them to the social clubs at Claremont, and there was no way on God's earth that I'd endure another brutal hell week and initiation. I'd heard that hazing was worse in fraternities than in our social clubs.

We crossed the room to the bar where a guy poured beer from a keg into plastic cups. We took the first cup of many to follow. Brad bragged that his goal for the night was to get lucky with a college girl. Randy wished him good luck but cautioned that he might get his butt kicked if he hit on a fraternity brother's girlfriend.

I continued to drink and take in the party's action. The party grew louder and wild as the crowd increased. Everyone was drinking and dancing and appeared to be having a good time. The noise and smoke were stifling. It was hard to move. I felt tipsy and wandered outside for fresh air. I'd forgotten my coat, and the cool night air chilled my body and my teeth chattered. Others had abandoned the party and milled in the parking lot. I was nauseated and slipped from view to an alley beside the building to throw up.

After relieving my stomach of numerous beers and a McDonald's supper, my body shook from the cold, and I stepped out to return to the party. Something quickly caught my attention, and I realized that two police cars entered the lot and stopped in front of the party hall.

"Ah, shit," I whispered and backed slowly into the alley. "This can't be happening," I sighed. "We'll be grounded for life if we get arrested."

The music and crowd noise came to an abrupt halt. I remained in the alley, my body shaking as the temperature continued to drop. The wait became an eternity. I heard voices and dared to steal a glance. I spotted the officers return to the cruisers, talking with two fraternity members. They shook hands, and I heard an audible "thank you" given by one of the students. "Thank God," I sighed, stepping into the open. I returned to the party to locate my missing friends.

The music returned, but at a much lower level. The chatter grew louder. I spotted Randy at the bar and joined him.

"What happened? Why were the police here?" I asked.

"Cops came and said to lower the music. They heard it on the highway. It's routine for the police to break up fraternity parties. They make themselves visible, check it out, and leave if there's no trouble. They usually don't bust the parties and arrest college students because it looks bad for the university. If everything is under control, they leave the partiers alone. They're cool with the fraternities."

"Man, I was petrified that we might get arrested. My parents would kill me," I claimed.

"Mine, too, but they weren't looking for trouble. Here, have another beer." He held a beer toward me.

"No, I've had my limit," I replied, realizing the odor was making me sick again. "Where's Brad?"

"I don't know. I haven't seen him for a while."

I took a 360 view of the room and didn't locate him, but it was difficult because of the poor lighting.

"How long are we staying?" I asked.

"Another hour. They have to shut down at midnight," he replied, checking his watch.

"Okay. I'll scout around and see if I find him."

I needed to get away from the bar and acrid smell of beer. I circled the room and checked the dance floor, but no Brad. I wasn't worried but admitted that we were twins for the weekend. If he got into trouble, I was in trouble, and vice versa. He was more likely, however, to find trouble than me.

The party ended. The lights were turned on, and the DJ removed his equipment from the room. Randy, his sister and her boyfriend, and I stood at the exit when Brad and a cute coed appeared.

"Where have you been?" Randy asked, obviously upset.

"Debbie was showing her Mustang to me." Both he and Debbie giggled.

"She's a freshman at Tech," he added, his clothes and hair disheveled.

"They want to lock up. We need to go," the boyfriend

said.

"Okay. I'll walk Debbie to her car and meet you at yours," Brad replied.

Our first college experience ended. Although the police incident created momentary fear, it was a good night. I pried Brad for the goods on Debbie later.

I dozed most of the return trip to Knoxville the next day. My parents asked how the weekend went, and I replied merely that it was "okay."

My dad asked, "Are you adding Tech to your potential college list?"

"I don't believe so," I replied. I never saw the campus.

Football season ended in November because Claremont finished 7-3 and didn't make the playoffs. Brad was upset because he wanted to win the state championship his senior year. Basketball season commenced, and dances resumed at the Armory on Saturday nights following home games. I no longer depended on others for rides since I had a car. My friends asked me for rides.

Brad played basketball, and with practice and a more than 20-game season, I didn't see him much until Spring when the season ended. High school thus far had been a whirlwind, and with my last high school Christmas approaching, I was bored. I delayed applying to colleges and universities for as long as I could, and the holiday break provided the opportunity to complete the process. I took both the SAT and ACT because some institutions required the SAT and others the ACT. My scores were in the middle range, which eliminated my admission to top schools.

I decided to get away from home and start fresh elsewhere. I applied to the University of North Carolina, Vanderbilt, Memphis State University, and Mercer College in Georgia. Due to my heavy co-curricular involvement at

Claremont, I developed an interest in politics and decided to major in political science and attend law school. Finances were an issue, and I hoped to earn scholarships and apply for a National Defense Loan. The Key Club scholarship was helpful.

I was in the last class to receive the college deferment for the draft, and I registered for the draft in March and endured the wait for the next draft lottery. My anger persisted over the Vietnam War. When Skip was killed, I claimed I would defect to Canada if drafted, but my feelings mellowed, realizing that I couldn't abandon my family.

I met with my guidance counselor and discussed my college choices. She was cautiously kind without hurting my feelings but hinted that I would have difficulty being admitted to the University of North Carolina and Vanderbilt. I informed her my back-up to law school was journalism, and I wanted to apply for the Grantland Rice Scholarship offered by Vanderbilt. She suggested that I apply to the University of Tennessee as a fifth choice, which I did. I developed an excellent relationship with my counselor and fully trusted advice she provided.

Memphis State became my first choice because it was far from home, and I enjoyed my brief visit to Memphis on our trip to California. My counselor encouraged that I delay my decision until hearing about scholarship and loan opportunities from the University of Tennessee. I agreed, realizing that UT was a mere ten miles East of my house.

I asked Brad about his college plans. We were aware that our college plans may be derailed because college deferments were eliminated. In November 1969, the Vietnam War worsened, and President Nixon signed an executive order to reinstate the draft. The first lottery held on December 1 covered men born from 1944 to 1950. The lottery in which Brad was eligible was held on July 1, 1970, and he was fortunate to have a relatively high number of 248. Numbers 195 and above were safe.

    Brad's dream was to be awarded a scholarship and play college football or basketball, although he confessed that his chance of getting a scholarship most likely would come from a small college. I begged him to apply to Memphis State and UT in case he didn't get scholarship offers. "We can be roommates," I said. I wanted to continue our friendship through college and recognized that if we went separate ways, it would end the close relationship we shared. He didn't appear to be overly excited about the idea and replied that he would think about it and let me know.

19

New Year's Eve 1969 was one of those nights I prefer to forget. Sue Davis and I were friends since junior high school. We served as each other's counselor when the need arose. Whereas Brad was my male alter ego, Sue offered advice and caring on the feminine side. She battled various adolescent issues, and we discussed our concerns and problems on a regular basis. My parents finally installed a phone in my room, and we spent many late nights calming and reassuring each other.

I viewed her as stunning. She had an exotic appearance and always moved with grace and dignity. Her parents were well off, and they lived in a gorgeous Tudor house on Kingston Pike. The landscape featured numerous cherry blossom trees and red rose bushes. It was the type of house I dreamed of owning one day. I spent much time at her house and developed a close relationship with her parents. To some extent, I was jealous that she had such cool parents. Sue worked harder than anyone on Brad's and my campaign committee.

Her parents were out for the evening at a New Year's Eve party at Cherokee Country Club. She invited a few friends to ring in the new year at her house. I asked Brad to join me, but he said he planned to party with his Kings brothers. I wasn't disappointed because I realized it was one of the last opportunities for him to be with the Kings before his graduation in June.

Sue's driveway was lined with cars when I arrived. She greeted me with a kiss on the cheek and asked what I wanted to drink. Several bottles of hard liquor covered the kitchen counter, and beer was in the refrigerator. I selected a Michelob. The evening was relatively calm with The 5th Dimension's *Aquarius/Let the Sunshine In* playing in the background and a small group enjoying the laid-back atmosphere. It was rather somber for a New Year's party, but no one seemed to mind. The night was young. Thirty minutes into the party, the doorbell sounded, and to my surprise, Brad entered. He spoke with Sue, and she offered him a drink. He accepted a beer and joined us in the living room and greeted the guests.

We hit our bottles together in a toast and said, "Happy New Year."

"What changed your mind?" I asked.

"The guys are going to a party in Alcoa, and I don't want to go that far and return after midnight when drunks will be on the road."

"How'd you get here?"

"They dropped me off. Thanks for inviting me to the party. I didn't want to spend New Year's at home."

"No problema, amigo. Do you know everyone?"

"Nah, but I will make my way around. You know me. I'm not shy."

"That's an understatement."

I shot a glance at the other kids in the room and noticed that eyes were turned toward Brad, obviously surprised that he was at the party. I was glad he came. If I drank too much, he would have to drive us home in my car.

There was an abundant supply of alcohol. Even though we were minors, everyone had a means of obtaining booze. A few of my friends had fake IDs. I was afraid to get one but remained aware that anytime I wanted booze, it was easy to obtain. Tennessee had a simple driver's license that was easy to change with an eraser and pen.

The doorbell rang again, and another of Sue's male friends entered with two guys she didn't know. The three were loud and appeared intoxicated. I watched as Sue confronted her friend and overheard her exclaim, "I don't want any trouble,

Bart."

Bart placed his arm around her shoulders and replied, "Don't worry. I've got everything under control."

One of Bart's friends, Mike, began a discussion with one of the girls. He was loud and other guests stared at him. Mike placed his hand on her shoulder, and she pushed him away. The guests recognized the worsening situation and hoped it would pass, but another attempt led the girl to soundly request that he leave her alone and go away, but he persisted. He reeked of alcohol and was dressed more for a camping trip than a nice party. This evening brought an end to Sue's friendship with Bart. Later, I prayed the same didn't also apply to me.

Sue approached Mike and asked him to please leave. "Where's Bart?" she shouted, searching the room.

Brad's patience was challenged, and he tired of Mike's obnoxious behavior. He approached Mike and grabbed his arm and said, "Back off, asshole."

Mike responded, "Fuck off." He turned back to the girl and said, "What's your name?"

Brad pulled his arm again, and Mike turned and slugged Brad hard in the jaw, knocking him to the floor. Brad hit an end table, causing a lamp to fall. The bulb popped, darkening the area.

Brad sprang to his feet, ready to pounce. Blood dripped from his nose onto the carpet. The guests stood in stunned silence, unaware of how to respond. Brad slammed his fist into Mike's face, briefly stunning him. Mike clinched his fist but was grabbed by Bart and his other friend who tightly held him.

"Get out of my house!" Sue yelled.

The two forcibly dragged their friend from the premises. "I'm not through with you," Mike warned Brad. Brad considered responding but decided he had caused enough damage.

Sue turned to me and said, "I believe you and Brad should leave, too."

I was disappointed and ashamed by the trail of events. My New Year's Eve was ruined. I was angry with Brad even though he responded as he believed he should. I asked Sue for a bag of ice for Brad's face before apologizing and leaving. I glanced out the window to make sure Bart and his friends were gone.

"Damn! Damn! Damn! Why does crap always happen to me? I was trying to help her, not cause a problem. I didn't know the son-of-a bitch was going to hit me," Brad exclaimed, striking my dashboard.

"Cool it!" I shouted. "You'll crack my dash. You look bad enough already. How's your hand?"

"Hurts like hell." He pulled down the visor and eyed his face in the mirror. Already swelling and bruising, he would have an ugly shiner the next day.

"What are you going to tell your parents?" I asked.

"I'm not worried about them. It's what coach will say that bothers me. I may be up shit creek."

We gathered our thoughts, and I flipped on the radio. I recognized Guy Lombardo playing *Aude Ang Sign*. The dashboard clock read 12:10. We missed New Year's. We heard the blasting of fireworks as we drove home. Their brilliant colors brightened the cold sky in the distance. The temperature was in the low 40s. I wished it was colder and would snow. I don't remember it ever snowing on New Year's Eve.

My mind was racing with too many thoughts about how the evening was ruined. Why did I invite Brad to the party? What would Sue's parents say? Was my relationship with them and Sue over? Would Mike and Brad have another confrontation? Probably not because he doesn't go to Claremont.

"Are your parents home?" Brad inquired, breaking my thoughts.

"No, they went to a party."

"Good, let's go to your house. I'll hang there until my parents go to bed, and then I'll sneak in. No reason to face them tonight. It can wait until morning."

"You can spend the night if you want," I offered.

"No, I don't want to explain what happened to your parents in the morning. No reason for you to get in trouble, too." He paused. "I'm really sorry, man. I'll call Sue tomorrow and apologize."

"You'd better not. I'll take care of it."

We spent an hour icing Brad's face and hand. He looked as though he was hit by a truck. I considered calling Sue but concluded it was a bad idea. The call could wait until the following day. Brad developed a strategy for informing his parents and coach what happened. He decided to tell his parents the truth because he truly believed he did what was right, although they ultimately viewed it differently. They asked why it was any of his business to confront Mike and that Sue was responsible for handling the situation. They were her guests. He was in a no-win situation.

January 1 fell on Thursday, and classes usually resumed after the Christmas break on January 2. The school board members, when setting the calendar for the year, concluded that returning for one day on Friday was useless, and January 2 was made part of the holiday. That worked in Brad's favor, giving his hand recuperation time, but his face worsened with the yellow bruising turning deep purple.

After much thought and discussion with his parents, he decided to be truthful with his coach and not dig himself into a deeper hole. The possibility existed for him to be penalized for bad behavior outside school, but his coach gave him a break for defending the young woman and being truthful. His penalty was running extra laps after practice and sitting out the first quarter of the next game against Clinton.

He was the luckiest person I knew.

....

1970 arrived. My last term in high school. Hopefully it was the last time I lived at home full-time. For the most part, high school was a success story, and I wanted to make the most of my remaining months. My peers couldn't wait to graduate, but I dreaded an unknown future without the friends I'd made and the good times we shared.

The next three months proved to be overly occupied with routine activities and new projects. We won the district in basketball but lost the first game in the regional tournament to Kingsport Dobyns-Bennett. Brad played superbly and was named the MVP of the district tournament. He developed a steady relationship with Melanie Underwood, a cheerleader. Between basketball practices and games and Melanie, I saw little of Brad. I continued to lead the Senior Class Steering Committee.

Much to my chagrin, I registered for the draft in March. The lottery for men born in 1952 was not held until Summer 1971, at which time I had completed my freshman year of college. Even if I had a low number, I had the last deferment and wouldn't be drafted and forced to leave college. For some reason, I was still nervous about the drawing. Fate was on my side, however, when the number drawn for my birthday was 149.

That was an anxious day for my parents and me when we endured the lingering and stressful drawing of 366 blue, plastic balls. Numbers up to 125 were called for the draft, and I was freed from the fear that if the war worsened, I could be pulled from college. I wasn't anti-military but anti-Vietnam

War, which I believed was an abomination. Even before Skip died, I didn't understand why we were there and what we were fighting for. I decided I would never go to war. Janie called to offer congratulations on my relatively high number.

20

Spring Break couldn't arrive soon enough. I was exhausted with the abundance of activities in which I was involved, heading the Senior Class Steering Committee, applying to colleges, and maintaining passing grades to insure graduation. My last high school activity was a service trip to Costa Rica with other Key Club members. Money raised by club members the past year helped with expenses, and we were responsible for our air flight. Financing was available for ten members, but only eight agreed to spend Spring Break dedicated to environmental work.

I deliberated extensively if I wanted to forfeit my last Spring Break of high school instead of partying with my friends. Besides the futile Mexico trip, I had never been out of the United States. It might be years before I had another opportunity. My parents were hesitant but realized that I would leave home for college in less than six months, and they had to adjust to losing me. They provided the airfare as a Christmas present. I applied for my passport and was set to go.

Was I truly going to make this trip without Brad? We shared adventures in Gatlinburg, Mexico, California, and Cookeville, and this might be the last opportunity for one final outing together. Luck again favored Brad when one of the guys going on the trip withdrew a month before departure.

I approached Terry Dorcey, the Key Club president, and the faculty advisor about Brad filling the vacant space. Both were hesitant because Brad wasn't a club member and hadn't participated in the fundraising activities. I argued that Brad proved his loyalty to the school through athletics and serving as senior class president and made several trips with us to the psychiatric hospital to play with the kids. He had an impeccable reputation and would be an asset on the trip. The two agreed Brad could go but based on a vote of the others making the trip. I considered that fair but needed to develop a plan to convince Brad.

Basketball season was over. It was a school night, and I knew Brad was home. I walked to his house to pose the proposition in person. His mother greeted me and said he was studying in his room. I opened the door and entered.

"Hey, dip shit, didn't your mother teach you manners about knocking first? I could have been spanking my monkey!" he said.

"That's your favorite pastime," I laughed.

"What the hell are you doing here?"

"I have a proposal for you!"

He accepted my interruption and placed his pencil on his desk. "I'm dying in anticipation," he laughed.

Brad was aware that I planned to spend Spring Break performing environmental work in the rain forest in Costa Rica and badgered me about forfeiting my final week of freedom in high school. I explained the Costa Rica trip and the opportunity for us to have a final hurrah before graduating and departing for college. I mentioned the only remaining obstacle was a vote by the others making the trip.

"That's not the only obstacle," he replied. "There are several—my parents, money, no passport, and Melanie."

"Your parents haven't said no to anything we've done. The cost is $400. Tell them you'll repay them from money you'll get as graduation gifts. I'll loan the money if you need it. You can pay an extra fee to get your passport on an emergency basis. And Melanie, well, I can't help you with her. You're on your own. It's only for a week, and if she cares for you, she'll wait."

"Easier said than done. It's Spring Break, and that means she'll have to find shit to do all week without me."

"Your call. The ball's in your court."

"It's a hard decision. I need to think about it."

"You can't take too long. You've got a tight time frame to get on board."

I was pleased with the outcome. The club members voted to allow Brad to join us. They knew and liked him and were excited that he desired to join us. His parents agreed to the trip, his passport arrived, and Melanie's parents decided to take the family to Myrtle Beach for Spring Break, thus becoming a non-issue.

Saturday, March 7 arrived, and we flew from Knoxville to Miami, to San José, Costa Rica for the start of our week's journey in this beautiful country. None of us slept much the night prior to departure due to anxiety and the early flight from Knoxville, resulting in catching up on sleep on both legs of the flights to San José. We cleared customs and rushed to pay phones to make calls to our parents that we arrived safely. We didn't have the opportunity to call home again until we returned to San José at week's end.

Our hosts greeted us at the airport in a large van and drove to a hostel where we spent the night. The weather was hot and humid, the opposite of the cool Spring weather we left hours earlier. As we traveled to the hostel, I was glued to my van window, absorbing the environs. The houses and buildings were painted various bright colors of blue, purple, pink, and green. Many of the houses had security bars on the windows and doors and locked steel gates. It reminded me of what we experienced in Tijuana.

We arrived at the hostel, which also bore barred windows and a locked gate. Our host gained entrance, and we grabbed our luggage and entered the facility. We were directed to our room, barren except for five bunk beds. The window was open, and a paper-thin curtain flapped in the breeze. I quickly realized the building was not air-conditioned. There was a small kitchen and one bathroom. I appreciated we were there for only one night. I wasn't aware we'd return there our last night in San José. Our group was housed in one room, and Brad and I shared a bunk bed.

We were warned to drink only container water because our systems were not used to the local water and drinking it might result in severe diarrhea and stomach cramps. I did not want my week ruined from getting sick, and I stuck with container water and strayed from anything containing ice or washed with the water.

Our travel mates left to tour the facility. I glanced at Brad and saw the gloom that engulfed his face. He looked as though he suffered a death in the family.

"What's wrong?" I asked.

"What the hell have you gotten me into?"

"Chill. This is just for one night. We leave for the rain forest tomorrow."

"This feels like a homeless shelter. I can't believe you talked me into this disaster. I could be home, sleeping until noon, hitting the pool all day, and partying at night."

I, too, was skeptical, but replied, "It'll get better. I promise. Give it a chance."

"It certainly isn't La Jolla," he joked.

"I agree, but nothing we do will ever beat La Jolla. That was a God-send opportunity."

Our hosts believed it was important for us to experience the country before beginning our work in the rain forest. They wanted us to develop an appreciation that touched our hearts and souls, one that would remain with us for the rest of our lives. They held deep pride in Costa Rica and spoke endlessly about its beauty and other assets. The national soccer team was a major source of honor.

After check-in, we drove to the mountains and had lunch at Restaurante Mi Terra. It was a typical Latin lunch, but more than I normally eat for dinner. I devoured my first black beans and rice and plantains. I predicted the beans would haunt me later, and I pitied the guys sharing the room with me.

Costa Rica is a land of volcanos. We traveled through Cartago to the Irazu Volcano National Park to visit Costa Rica's highest active volcano, Irazu. The weather was cool and foggy, and our guide advised us to bring a jacket. The fog was thick and made it difficult to experience a proper view of the Craters Diego and De La Haya. We investigated the area and took a group photograph.

Our next stop was in nearby Orosi Valley, whose Colonial Orosi Church, is the oldest Catholic church still in operation in Costa Rica. Built in 1735, I was stunned by its architectural detail and beauty. I entered and knelt at a pew to absorb the serenity of the occasion. As a Catholic, my mother taught me that anytime I visited a Catholic church for the first time, I should make three wishes. I did so, wishing for a safe Spring Break, the end of the Vietnam War, and good health and safety for my family and friends.

The church was surrounded by hills and lush vegetation. The humidity was stifling. My shirt was wet with perspiration, and my thirst was unbearable. A small carnival filled the street near the church, and Brad and I bought our first churros and canned cold drinks. His mood perked since departing the hostel. He was a kid from a small town in Iowa, and he had never experienced anything like he had seen and undergone in a mere twenty-four hours. I admit that the same sentiment was true for me.

We returned to Cartago and made a final stop at the Basilica de Los Angeles. A mass was in progress and we were unable to tour the ancient church built in 1639. I was disappointed but exhausted from the extremely long day and anxious for a good night's sleep. We returned to our van and spotted a huge wagon on display in a fenced area. Terry Dorsey had several years of Spanish classes to his credit and assumed the role of official translator. He read the display sign and informed us that the wagon was called a *carreta*, a type of wagon pulled by a horse and used on farms in the nation's older days.

We returned to San José and enjoyed dinner at a Mexican restaurant. I ate lightly in fear of having stomach problems from a late, spicy meal. With only one restroom at the hostel, our late night was extended as we took turns using the restroom and showering.

"Holy shit!" Brad exclaimed, entering the room in his underwear, and drying his hair. "There is no hot water. Just cold. And there's not much water pressure. I was freezing my ass off." I was the last to shower and quickly learned that Brad's outcry was truthful.

It was a good day, and I enjoyed the group of Key Club members on the trip. Brad fit in well, and I hoped he maintained a positive attitude for the remainder of the week. I felt responsibility for him since I convinced the group to allow him on the trip.

We ate a hearty breakfast of eggs, plantains, black beans, rice, and coffee. It was the first time I had black beans and rice for breakfast. I quickly learned they were served with every meal.

We loaded the van and were filled with excitement that our journey to the rain forest had finally arrived. We stopped at a supermarket to buy soft drinks, water, and snacks for the coming week. We departed the city and traversed the winding roads into the mountains, passing tiny hamlets filled with residents performing their daily routines. Nine years later, this area would boast the San Luis Canopy zip lining tour, an activity we would have been thrilled to experience, especially Brad.

Rain slowed our journey to our destination, but after three hours, we drove twenty miles beyond Bijagua to the Volcan Tenorio National Park, where a forest ranger's station housed us for the next five days. The Guanacaste mountain range is beautiful, and I attempted to compare it to the Great Smokey Mountains, but there is a distinct difference. Each possesses its own unique characteristics, blanketed in natural beauty.

We checked into the ranger's station and were shown to our room, cramped with five sets of bunk beds. There was no air conditioning, but we didn't expect it in the rain forest. There was one window and a floor fan to help ease the dry, sticky nights. I thanked God we were blessed with electricity. The facility had two restrooms and two showers, offering only ice-cold water. A cook staffed the kitchen and prepared three daily meals.

We learned upon arrival that a high school group of ten, including their advisor, from Mobile, Alabama joined us for the week. It was a coed group, which brought quick, bright smiles to our all-male group.

Following lunch, the head ranger, in badly broken English, provided an introduction and overview of the park and our week's assignment. The heat was unbearable, and I struggled to stay awake during the session. Brad's attention often drifted to viewing the girls from Mobile. I worried that there would be a problem if Brad tried to hook up with one of the coeds.

Our assignment for the week was to help construct steps on a steep hill leading to the Rio Celeste, with amazing light blue water, caused by the emanation of sulfur and the precipitation of calcium carbonates. Once the steps were completed, visitors could trek to the base of a beautiful waterfall and soak in the stunning environment of flora and fauna species, disturbed only by the water rushing from the falls to the bottom.

We commenced a four-hour hike following the orientation session. To experience first-hand the difficult task at hand for the week, we struggled down the steep incline leading to the waterfall, holding onto tree limbs to keep from falling, sliding in the mud, and noting that a bad slip could result in a serious fall down the hillside. The trip convinced us that steps were needed for future tourists to safely complete the journey.

We continued our hike through the amazing rain forest. We packed sandwiches and drinks and stopped after two hours to eat. We joined the students from Mobile to get acquainted. Brad immediately attached himself to a striking blue-eyed blonde with a rather deep southern accent. I wondered if Melanie had attached herself to a stalking blonde-hair stud at the beach on her Spring Break. The two groups quickly formed a bond and anticipated the challenge that awaited us. We admitted that working with the cute southern belles would make the work less strenuous and perhaps even enjoyable.

The hike was exhausting, and we didn't return to the ranger station until after dark. I considered myself in good shape but feared I'd be sore the next day. We had a late dinner and crashed early because the morning call for breakfast came at seven, followed by the first hard day of work.

I cornered Brad briefly after dinner and said, "Be careful in starting anything with that hot chick. Don't create a bad situation for us. I vouched for you with the club members and said that you wouldn't cause any problems."

"I'm cool, bro. You don't have to worry about me."
"That's the problem. Yes, I do."
"Chill. I'm just being friendly. No other intentions."
"If only that were true," I replied with sarcasm.
"By the way, did you bring a rubber?" he seriously asked and then laughed.
"You're an ass," I said, striking hard on his shoulder.

....

I couldn't remember a time that I had worked that hard, not even for Mr. Erickson. We moved gravel from a large pile to the top of the hill where the steps began. We moved it by wheelbarrow, and when that became too cumbersome, we switched and formed a human chain and passed bags filled with gravel. The thick trees completely shaded us, blocking the glazing sun, but the humidity remained high. Lunch break couldn't arrive soon enough.

The day's work was completed by 4:00 and we finished to shower and rest before dinner. A heavy thunderstorm hit prior to dinner and knocked out the power, forcing us to eat by lantern light. We played Monopoly and card games with our new friends, but thoroughly exhausted from the day's work, we were in bed by 10:00.

We began construction on the steps the next day. Two men hired by the rangers to assist us demonstrated how to build the steps. Since the forest is protected, we weren't allowed to cut trees or disturb natural objects. We searched for dead trees to gather branches, which were used to brace the gravel-covered steps. My back ached from leaning to spread gravel and hammer the stick braces into the soft mud. We were too busy to converse, but suddenly a loud scream sounded, "La culebra!"

We stopped work and turned toward the local worker who chopped at the ground with his machete.

"It's a viper," Terry Dorcey explained.

I was aware that vipers are poisonous snakes. I had never seen one and was curious. I asked Terry to inquire if the snake was dead and could we see it?

"La serpienta esta viva o muerta?"

"Si, muerta."

"Podemos verlo?"

"Si," he waved us over.

Most of the students didn't want to see it, but I joined several others in eyeing the dead reptile. When reminiscing about the trip at home, I bragged that I saw a viper. I didn't admit it was dead but eventually confessed that a worker killed it.

Something didn't settle well with my stomach from food I ate that day. At 3:00 in the morning, I was awakened by the sudden need to rush to the restroom. I had a case of Montezuma's Revenge. Little sleep was had because I made several trips before the morning call for breakfast.

I was supplied diarrhea medicine and declined to eat anything at breakfast. Working that day was out of the question. I remained behind to recuperate. I was angry and disappointed. I didn't want to be called a wimp, although that was the first word Brad said to me when he heard I was sick.

"You're just trying to get out of work, wimp," he said. "You can't take hard work, you big baby."

"Screw you," I replied. "You could have a little sympathy."

He responded by pretending to play a tiny violin.

I was better the following day and returned to the project. We reached the half-way point of the path and stopped work early. The rangers informed us that they had arranged for us to walk to the neighboring town and play a soccer game with the local kids. The news excited us, mostly for stopping work early. Soccer had yet to make its way to the U.S. to become a competitive sport. None in my group had played, but we looked forward to spending time with the locals and learning a new sport.

We returned to the ranger station to change clothes and eat lunch. We hurried through the meal because we were excited to meet the kids and play soccer. We walked a half-mile along a dirt road to a well-manicured soccer field adjacent to a school. A dozen kids who appeared to be ages ten to sixteen were kicking soccer balls around the field, awaiting our arrival. We told the ranger that we didn't know how to play, and he explained the rules as best he could. Terry translated. Terry spoke to one of the older boys and explained that he was the only one in our group who spoke Spanish. The girls from Mobile didn't want to play and stood on the sidelines and cheered for us.

Brad was in heaven. He was the happiest I'd seen him since leaving Knoxville. He befriended one of the teenagers and practiced his newly acquired skills. Being a natural athlete, he quickly adapted to the new sport and played as though he'd played his entire life. I also learned quickly and believed I found a sport that I could master. I was a runner, and soccer requires constant running and endurance.

I wish that I could say the game was close, but we were beaten by more than ten goals, although our hosts had mercy on us and didn't keep score. Brad and one of the Key Clubbers scored two goals for our team. I believe the kids may have felt sorry for us and allowed us to score. It was a fun afternoon, and I believe the local kids had as much fun as we, particularly beating the gringos.

Exhaustion overcame us. Following dinner, we chatted with the Mobile students in the dining hall. The blonde from Mobile rose and walked toward her wing of the building. Brad, sitting next to me, waited a minute and rose. It took only a second for me to realize what he was up to.

"Where are you going?" I asked

"What's it to you? I have to pee."

"Me, too," I stood and joined him.

"We're not going together, Steve. The guys will talk."

"Let 'em. Let's go."

"Screw it. I'll wait." He sat noisily, causing the others to glance our way.

"My mother didn't raise no fool," I replied, sitting.

"You're not my babysitter, Jackson." He was angry, but I didn't care.

Our last workday came and went. We grew accustomed to the back-breaking routine and our muscles no longer ached from the strenuous work. A heavy rain fell, resulting in a cool night's sleep. Brad avoided me in the morning and sat with his new blonde friend at breakfast. We said goodbyes with hugs and address and phone exchanges and readied for our return trip to San José.

It was an amazing week, and along with the trip to California, it became one of the best times of my young life. We made the long trip back to San José in the non-air-conditioned van. We experienced a lengthy delay because of a serious accident on a bridge we needed to cross. We were required to pull to the side of the road and wait two hours for the accident to clear. It was too hot to sit in the van, so we exited and sat under trees to avoid the heat.

Several hours later, we arrived at the hostel where we dropped our luggage and hurried to our dinner reservation at Restaurante Nuestra Tierra. It offered real authentic Costa Rican cuisine, and we longed for an excellent meal our last night. We slept well because of the long day and sitting in the stifling hot sun while the accident cleared.

We waited turns to endure the cold shower in the morning, packed bags, and loaded the van. Our hosts insisted that we have a nice, traditional breakfast and took us to a restaurant in San José. My favorite part of the meal was the amazing coffee.

Following the heavy breakfast, we visited the National Theater, which was built in the 1890s. It is an impressive and beautiful structure. Next was a tour of the National Museum, which originally was built as a fort. We had lunch and finished the afternoon shopping for souvenirs at the Arts and Crafts Market. I bought t-shirts for Dad and me and a religious trinket for my mother.

The trip was one of the highlights of my high school years. I learned to appreciate the beautiful country and its people. Even though it has riches, it possesses pockets of poverty, which increased my appreciation of the amazing life I had in the United States. I'll never forget the experience of contributing to the amazing rain forest environment and leaving it better than we found it. I learned to appreciate new foods and experience architecture older than the United States. One of the highlights was learning to play soccer with the local kids in a desolate area of Bijagua.

By the time we boarded the plane, Brad and I were friends again. Between naps on both legs of our flights to Knoxville, we reviewed the entire week. Brad said that for the second time in his life, he owed me big time. He agreed it was an unforgettable experience. He loved the exercise the hard work provided. His favorite part of the week was learning to play soccer. We didn't mention the blonde from Mobile.

Pura Vida!

21

Spring was filled with school activities, weekend parties, attending track meets, and completing college applications. As predicted, I was denied admission to Vanderbilt and the University of North Carolina and accepted by Tennessee, Mercer, and Memphis State. I earned several scholarships and a National Defense Loan and ultimately chose Tennessee, with my stipulation that I live on campus and not commute from home. I entered a Knoxville Optimistic Club essay contest, "Patriotic Citizenship Needs Optimism," and won a $250 prize for first place, which I deposited in my college fund. Terry Dorcey helped with my decision to attend Tennessee by offering to room together on campus.

Brad was vague when I asked him about his application process. He replied that he was waiting to hear from colleges about an athletic scholarship. I believed he was living a dream. He was a good athlete, but not good enough for a football or basketball scholarship offer from a large university. His chances were better at smaller colleges like Maryville, East Tennessee State, or Carson-Newman.

Our attention was consumed in April with the aborted Apollo 13 mission to the moon. Astronauts Jim Lowell, Jack Swigert, and Fred Haise struggled to repair equipment damage which threatened their oxygen supply. We watched the news for two days, praying for a safe return. Using masking tape, maps, and miscellaneous supplies in the capsule, they temporarily solved the issue, rounded the moon, and headed to earth. On April 17, they successfully splashed down in the South Pacific Ocean.

....

Billy Graham was America's pastor. He was the most renowned and successful evangelist in the world. His worldwide crusades drew hundreds of thousands of people. When a Knoxville crusade was announced for May, I jumped at the opportunity to attend. My parents cited our Catholic religion as the reason they had no interest in attending but said I was free to go. They complained that traffic would be a nightmare and had no desire to sit in it for hours to listen to a hillbilly preacher from North Carolina.

My next move was to ask Brad to go with me. I was batting one thousand in convincing Brad to join me on several adventures, and now an opportunity arose to add one more to the list.

Graham's ten-day crusade was held at the University of Tennessee's Neyland Stadium. I chose to attend May 24 when Johnny Cash was a featured guest. I wasn't a country music fan but liked Cash. I convinced Brad that the crusade was on Sunday and as seniors, we didn't have much homework close to graduation. He agreed to go if Melanie could join us. I had no problem with that, but her parents wouldn't allow her, and Brad grudgingly relented because he *owed me*.

Traffic was the mess my parents predicted. Parking was a nightmare, and after entering the huge facility, we located seats and joined more than 55,000 others gathered for the event. In press interviews, Rev. Graham said he was directing his message during the crusade to young people because of campus unrest across country where students protested the ongoing Vietnam War.

Cash sang *How Great Thou Art* and provided a testimonial for the crowd. Rev. Graham thanked him and welcomed everyone to beautiful Neyland Stadium and the University of Tennessee. It was a humid night, and spectators used various objects to fan themselves. Rev. Graham said he was pleased that so many young people were in attendance and proceeded to read *Bible* verses and directed his message to the youth of America. He proclaimed young people the future and said it was our responsibility to protect what so many who came before us had left. He declared that many individuals in the military made the ultimate sacrifice to guarantee our freedom.

The next day, it was announced that President Nixon would attend the crusade on Thursday. It was an opportunity for me to see a sitting president for the first time. Undoubtedly others planned to attend to see Nixon, not necessarily to hear Rev. Graham. Hundreds of protestors were expected that night.

A mere three weeks earlier on May 4, Ohio National Guardsmen used live ammunition to break up an anti-war demonstration on the Kent State University campus and killed four students and injured nine others. The guardsmen were sent to the campus by Governor Jim Rhodes. It was a disgraceful act of cowardice, and the country was in an uproar. The governor should have been held accountable, but he ultimately was found not responsible. Did this really happen on a college campus in America? It was a stunning and unforgiveable act of stupidity.

My charge was to convince my parents to allow me to attend again, particularly following the Kent State shootings, and on a school night. Since President Nixon would be there, they believed the rowdy protestors would create a dangerous environment. I told them that if I was a student at UT, they wouldn't know if I attended or not. After much pleading and agreeing to a long list of dos and don'ts, they relented with the condition that Brad join me. They insisted I couldn't go alone. That was not a problem because I intended to ask him all along.

Once I spoke to Brad, we agreed it best for my mother to speak to his mother. With all parties on board, we were given the okay but instructed to complete homework before we left.

The atmosphere outside and inside the stadium reminded me of what we experienced when we attended the memorial service for Rev. King. There was an eerie calm, which disappeared with bellowing shouts we heard when we arrived in the parking lot. Protestors surrounded the stadium, many holding signs reading, "Thou shall not kill." Police and security blanketed the area.

Once seated, we noticed that most protestors were restricted to the far end of the stadium away from the stage. The chants were loud and drowned out the preliminary speaker and George Beverly Shea's opening song. Before she sang *His Eye is on the Sparrow*, Ethel Waters chastised the protestors for their behavior. She said that if she was close enough, she'd smack them.

We were seated far from the stage and didn't have a good view of President Nixon and the First Lady, but I knew Nixon was there and was thrilled that I saw my first president in person. When I registered for the draft the following year, I also registered to vote, and in my first presidential election in 1972, I voted for Nixon over Sen. George McGovern of South Dakota. My parents were Democrats, but being a self-professed rebel, I registered as a Republican.

We couldn't hear Nixon's brief remarks because of the loud protestors, who quieted when Rev. Graham took the podium. Reiterating his intent to deliver a message to young people, he opened with two Biblical quotes, quoting First Isiah 40, verses 30 and 31, he read, "Even youths get tired and weary; even strong young men clumsily stumble. But those who wait for the Lords help find renewed strength; they rise up as if they had eagle's wings, they run without growing weary, they walk without getting tired."

"And we learn in First Timothy, 4:12," he quoted, "Let no man despise thy youth; but be thou an example of the believers, in word, in conversation, in charity, in spirit, in faith, in purity."

The service concluded with the gospel hymn, *Just As I*

Am. As the choir sang, Rev. Graham invited individuals in the crowd to come forward onto the field to the stage and accept Jesus Christ as their Savior or rededicate their lives to Christ. I watched as hundreds, perhaps thousands, trance-like, flooded the aisles. Brad and I weren't moved to join the herd of people and chose to leave and beat the heavy traffic.

Inching slowly West on Interstate 40, I asked Brad, "What did you think?"

No response. I asked again, "What did you think?"

"It's was ok. Nixon is an ass. It was a publicity stunt. He's in over his head with the war, and it's spreading to other countries. They shouldn't have mixed politics with religion. Graham lost a lot of credibility in my view."

I wasn't sure if I agreed or not, but I respected his opinion. "I'm definitely anti-war," I said, "but it was a no-win for Nixon. Damned if he does and damned if he doesn't. I believe there is a time and place for everything, and the protestors should have been more respectful. I've never seen so much security."

"Just exercising their free speech rights."

I didn't want to argue and replied, "Thanks for going. Like him or not, we can say we saw a U.S. president in person."

"Yeah, you're right, but no big deal for me."

I wasn't sure why he was in a sour mood and concluded the discussion. My parents taught me to never discuss politics or religion with friends or family. I turned on the radio, and The Beatles *Let It Be* filled the car. It seemed apropos. Little was said for the remainder of the ride.

Graduation was a week away. The years passed quickly. When I was young, all I wanted to do was grow up. Now, I wanted time to slow. There were various low periods during high school, but overall, I enjoyed the three years of academic challenges and frolicking outside the classroom. I made many life-long friends who helped me along the arduous way. I entered as a timid sophomore, seeking to define my future. I had the help of mentors who provided direction but ultimately allowed me to determine my fate. Peer pressure was immense, resulting in wise as well as regrettable decisions. Brad was there every step of the way.

Graduation was set for our football stadium, but rain forced the ceremony to be moved into cramped quarters in the school auditorium. Brad, our class treasurer, secretary, and I were privileged to join the principal, the superintendent, Congressman John Duncan, Sr., and other guests on stage. Brad and the class valedictorian were the student speakers.

Unlike his speech for class president, Brad didn't seek my help, and I didn't offer. He said Melanie helped him, which meant she wrote it.

He thanked the principal for his kind introduction and began,

"Fellow students, parents, and honored guests. This day has finally arrived. No more tests! (cheers) No more long essays! (more cheers) And no more cafeteria food! (laughter and loud cheers).

"As your president, I am proud of the class of 1970 and what we accomplished together. I thank my fellow officers for making me look good. I thank my teachers, counselors, and coaches for helping to build me into the person I've become.

"I don't deny that the past three years had challenges—for us as individuals and for our country (hinting at Vietnam). We students want our independence and freedom. This is a rite of passage into adulthood. For you parents, it's been a time to let go and to make new commitments to your son or daughter as a young adult. We thank you for giving us space (laughter).

"Regardless of what each of you do following graduation, treasure your independence and trust your judgment. Get involved and make a commitment to help others less fortunate than yourself. Most importantly, be happy.

"Please don't forget your alma mater. Come back for Knights' sporting events and the annual Homecoming game. Attend future class reunions.

"I leave you with this message about Robert Louis Stevenson, who wrote a couple of the books we read in English class. When he was a young boy, he sat by the window at dusk one evening watching the lamplighter as he walked by his house touching the gas wick to the gaslights on the street. His mother, concerned over the long period of silence, asked young Robert what he was doing. He replied, 'I am watching the man punch holes in the darkness.'

"Each of you can punch holes in the darkness and make a difference in the lives of others. I challenge you to do so!

"Thank you, Class of 1970! Good luck in your future endeavors and go Knights!"

The seniors, seated together, stood with resounding applause. We each shook Brad's hand as he soaked in the adulation. I was somewhat stunned at how well he presented his speech. He certainly sent the class out on a high note.

I beamed with pride and glanced slowly around the room, taking in the atmosphere, and appreciating the fact that this would be the last time we'd be together as a class. We would leave and go our separate ways, some with great success, and others with disappointing failure. It was an emotional moment. I asked myself, "Where did the time go?"

I anticipated a heavy night of drinking and informed my parents I was spending the night with Terry Dorcey. They met and trusted him and assumed we were destined to be college roommates. I anticipated partying with Brad and celebrating graduation and our years of friendship, but he had plans with Melanie.

Terry's sister hosted a graduation party with an abundance of alcohol for him and his friends, which surprised me because the guests were minors. My drink of choice for the evening was lime daiquiris. Even though I bragged to my friends about drinking, I didn't drink as much as I claimed, which usually was due to peer pressure. I was too young and inexperienced to recognize my limit, which was far exceeded that evening.

I remember making several pitchers of daiquiris but not much after that. I remember rushing out of the house to throw up. I don't know how long I was outdoors but became conscious of Terry assisting me back inside. I awoke before noon the following day with a sledgehammer pounding inside my head. It remains the worst hangover I've had. I was no longer nauseated because I had nothing left in my system. My bladder forced me to the bathroom, and I thanked God I hadn't peed my pants. My stomach required more revenge, and I knelt on the floor hugging the toilet while dry heaves had their way.

Terry stayed the night, too. I heard him and his sister talking in the kitchen, and with deep humility and embarrassment, I meekly joined them.

"The dead walks!" Terry laughed.

"I am so sorry," I said. "I don't know what came over me last night."

"A dozen daiquiris. Would you like another pitcher?"

I gave Terry a dirty look. I didn't appreciate his humor, and the thought almost caused me to rush to the bathroom again.

"Would you like something to eat?" Terry's sister offered.

"No thanks," I replied. "Not sure the food will settle well. I need a few hours."

My car was at Terry's and I didn't want my parents calling and asking for me, so I suggested to Terry that we leave. With another apology to his sister, we returned to his house.

The entire distance was painful. I remained dizzy and queasy. I feared Terry might have to pull over to allow me to vomit. Luck was with me, and we didn't stop. I retrieved my car after thanking and apologizing for the hundredth time and made the slow trek home.

The remainder of the day was spent on the couch, watching television. I wasn't naïve enough to assume my parents weren't aware of my condition. Graciously, they left me alone until supper.

22

One last Summer before heading to college. Brad and I celebrated several last hurrahs, and I asked myself, why not one more? What idea could we scheme together? Neither of us had a Summer job, which frustrated our parents.

Someone always came to the rescue, and in this case, it was Terry Dorcey. Terry was an Eagle Scout. I was in Cub Scouts at an early age, but when the den mother retired, the troop disbanded when no one assumed the responsibility.

Terry appeared desperate when he called a few days after graduation.

"You recover from graduation night?" he asked without humor.

"Yeah, it took a while. Never again," I said. "I can't stand the smell of anything lime. I wouldn't drink another lime daiquiri for a hundred bucks. What's up?"

"Do you have a Summer job?"

"No, and my parents aren't happy about it."

"I have a proposition for you."

I couldn't imagine what it could be and replied, "I'm listening."

"As you know, I'm an Eagle Scout, and for the past two Summers, I've worked at a Boy Scout camp. The director called today and said that he lost a couple of counselors and is desperate to find replacements. That's where you come in."

"I'm not a Boy Scout."

"I told him that, and it matters, but it doesn't in this situation. All you have to do is officially register with the national Boy Scout organization, and you're covered."

"Where's the camp?"

"It's in Jackson. It's a neat place on the lake. I've had a blast the past two years and can't wait to go again."

"Tell me more. What will I do?"

"You'll be a camp counselor like me. We have our own cabin. There's a mess hall with three meals a day. Each week a new group of Scouts arrive, and you'll be assigned two troops. There's a lake and canoes. We end the week with a big bonfire and award presentations. It's right up your alley. You were tremendous in Key Club, and this will far exceed that experience."

"What about pay?"

"It's not much, but you have zero expenses and will save everything you earn. We will have a cool time and prepare for our Fall together as roommates at UT."

"You said there's another opening. How about Brad?"

Terry hesitated and said, "There is another spot, but you know Brad. He gets wild, and can we trust him to stay out of trouble?"

"I know what you mean, Ter, but I will vouch for him. There won't be any girls there, so he won't be tempted to get into trouble. He didn't cause any problems in Costa Rica, and he was a huge hit with the kids at the psychiatric hospital."

A longer pause.

"If we weren't desperate, I'd say no. If we don't fill the spot, then the other counselors will be assigned additional troops, and that's too much work. I'll give in and speak in his behalf to the camp director, but you have to warn him about his behavior and keep a watch on him."

"I promise. I'll check with him and get back to you."

It took no convincing Brad to accept the offer. He welcomed the opportunity to get away from home for the Summer, frolic in the wilds with the Boy Scouts, and earn money. I warned him about the strict camp rules and to not embarrass me.

"Not to worry. I'll be an angel," he laughed.

"I won't hold my breath," I replied. "I'll get more information from Terry, and we need to tell our parents." I noted to myself that I said, *tell our parents* instead of *ask them*. We were leaving for college in three months, and the process of letting go should commence.

We arrived at camp several days early to endure hours of instructions and lessons about camp procedures and policies. The rules were strict. We had mandatory meals at 7:30 a.m., noon, and 5:00 p.m. Following the introduction sessions, we cleaned the camp sites and erected tents.

Our cabin was closed since the previous Summer and required a thorough cleaning. We provided cots in the tents for the Scouts and their leaders, and the counselors had beds in our cabin. We brought sheets and a pillow from home. The cabin had a bathroom with a toilet, sink, and shower that four of us shared. Unlike Costa Rica, we had hot water.

Brad proved his worth and impressed the staff with his hard work and dedication. He was quick to volunteer and went beyond the call of duty. Prior to arrival at camp, we purchased the required Boy Scout uniform consisting of shirt, shorts, long socks, and garters. The camp director provided us with the camp patch, and we struggled with the difficult task of sewing it on our shirtsleeve. Brad admitted he would be angry if any Kings saw him in a Boy Scout uniform and forbade me from taking pictures. I asked him why he gave a shit since we graduated and probably wouldn't see most of them again. He agreed but still refused to have his picture taken.

We worked our asses off preparing the camp for the Scouts' arrival. It was harder than the work in Costa Rica because we committed eight hours per day, breaking only for lunch. Following supper, we spent the nights reviewing materials and crashing early from exhaustion. I brought a transistor radio from home, but it didn't locate any stations due to the thick woods. Luckily, Terry brought an eight-track player and several tapes. Another counselor had a Led Zeppelin tape, and it played endlessly. I grew tired of hearing *Whole Lotta Love*. I was a Simon and Garfunkel fan and listened to one of their tapes. My favorite new group was Chicago and regularly played their first release, *Chicago Transit Authority*.

The first set of troops arrived on Sunday and remained until Saturday morning. We prepared the troops for the various activities of the week, including catching bugs or anything that could race in the critter crawl on Friday. Camp site inspections were held daily after breakfast when the Scouts departed for their assigned morning activities. The counselors split inspection duties. We walked to each campsite and completed a checklist of requirements. The camp had to be clean of debris, supplies neatly stacked, and tents in impeccable order. Points were deducted for violations. At the final bonfire Friday night, the troop with the highest point total for the week was given the Honor Troop Award. Three of my troops won the award over the course of Summer.

Terry was a certified lifeguard. He and another counselor handled the water activities and spent every day at the lake. I was jealous of their golden-brown tans and wished that I was a certified lifeguard. Water activities included canoeing, swimming, mile swim, and teaching the Scouts lifesaving and drown proofing. They also oversaw the water carnival held on Friday.

There were ten activities the Scouts could undertake during the week, and for each completed activity, a different color bead was awarded. Once all ten beads were earned, they were placed on a leather bracelet that the Scouts wore with pride. Although we didn't have time to be bored, I convinced

Brad that we should accept the challenge and complete the activities. Being an avid sportsman, Brad quickly accepted, and we undertook each task. Unlike the Scouts who had to finish by week's end, we completed them at our leisure.

The most difficult tasks were the mile swim and drown proofing. Terry explained that individuals stranded in the ocean remained alive for 24 hours thanks to drown proofing. The test required that we drown proof for one hour. I found it more difficult than the mile swim. It was boring and required keeping my eyes closed the entire time. I had no idea about time passage until Terry lifted me from the water and informed me that the hour had expired.

Since the mile swim and drown proofing required longer time, we couldn't take the time away from our duties and waited until the troops departed and completed them Saturday afternoon. Terry monitored us and followed in a canoe during the mile swim. I didn't have the confidence that I could swim a mile, but I was in better shape than I assumed and finished a few minutes behind Brad.

Two of the additional tasks were skeet shooting at the rifle range and target shooting with a bow and arrow. I'd never done either and was thrilled at the opportunity to attempt both.

We completed the tasks and placed the ten beads on our bracelets and wore them with pride the remainder of camp. They served as incentives for the Scouts who admired them and sought to earn one. Mine still resides somewhere in my boxes of treasured junk in my garage.

Friday night campfire was the week's highlight. We sang songs, held the critter crawl, presented awards, and cooked S'mores on a huge fire. One of the counselors played the guitar, and he and I memorized and sang Dion's *Abraham, Martin, and John*. We also wrote an original song about the camp to the tune of Peter, Paul, and Mary's *Old Stewball*, which was well received by the Scouts and Scoutmasters.

Mid-way through the fourth week, Terry became ill, had a fever, and was forced to remain in our cabin. The camp director asked Brad to assume Terry's position at the waterfront. He welcomed the opportunity to bathe in the hot sun all day. He wanted to impress the director and perform with perfection. The morning shift and the one-hour wait after lunch expired. Brad assumed the lifeguard duties while his partner supervised the canoers.

Brad carefully eyed each swimmer in the restricted swimming area. Something caught his attention, and he recognized a Scout drifting past the rope barrier. He blew his whistle. No response because the Scout's head was under water. Had he purposely gone beyond the barrier or did he not realize where he was? Brad continued to blow. The other counselor was too far from the swimmer to assist and couldn't leave the canoers.

The Scout disappeared under water and his hands frantically slapped the surface. Brad realized he was in trouble, blew the emergency call of three consecutive blasts on his whistle, and ran for the water. At the sound of the emergency whistle, other staff members ran to the water's edge. The Scouts that were swimming were forced onto the beach.

Brad swam with lightning speed to the distressed swimmer and pulled him to the surface. He held him away from his body in a tight grip so that the panicking Scout wouldn't pull him under. Brad skillfully grasped the youth under his left arm and swam to shore. He laid the kid on his side on the sandy beach so he could expel any remaining water. CPR wasn't necessary because the Scout was conscious. The Scout stood and hugged Brad. A crowd gathered. There was applause, and Brad received verbal congratulations and slaps on his back.

The camp director asked the young Scout if he was

okay and took him by the arm and departed for the camp nurse. The director was pleased with the happy ending but frustrated that the event required a written report to the district office and a call to the Scout's parents. He asked himself would the incident have occurred had Terry been on duty. Perhaps Terry would have called the Scout in before he drifted beyond the rope barrier. The director had second thoughts about leaving the water activities open once Terry fell ill and replacing him with a non-certified guard. It was a bunch of what ifs and was something he would deal with later.

Brad entered the mess hall for supper that evening and received a standing ovation. Normally glowing in the limelight, Brad appeared uncomfortable with the attention. He said he did what he was supposed to do. At Friday's campfire, the camp director announced that a new award was created and presented the Hero Award to Brad.

The last two days at camp were filled with removing everything we assembled three months earlier and storing it until next year. The camp director took us into town for pizza our last night.

Brad and I talked the entire return drive to Knoxville. He agreed that we add the camp experience to our growing list of the best times of our lives. We formed what we believed were lasting friendships; however, besides Terry, neither of us saw anyone from camp again. It eventually faded into another memory in the distant past.

23

I submitted my housing application late to UT, and Terry and I were assigned different residence halls, he to the air-conditioned Carrick Hall and me to the non-air-conditioned Hess Hall. We went our separate ways and never interacted on campus.

Brad decided to not apply to UT because he wanted to attend Cumberland College in Williamsburg, Kentucky, and attempt to walk-on for the basketball team. He failed to do well academically and dropped out after his freshman year. He missed Melanie badly, and the distance strained their relationship.

He returned home and couldn't locate a job. He refused to work at a fast-food restaurant and made the difficult decision to join the Army. His parents were devastated. He finally achieved his dream of skydiving, trained with the 82nd Airborne at Ft. Bragg, North Carolina, and was sent to Vietnam. Thoughts of Skip flooded my brain, and I worried intensely about his safety. I kept him in my prayers and don't know how I would have handled it had something happen to him. We corresponded, but not often. Brad wasn't a letter writer, although he regularly answered Melanie's letters.

He safely survived his tour of duty and finished his service requirement in Stuttgart, Germany. He and Melanie were married six months later, and I was his best man, which I considered an honor. I was happy he survived the war and married his high school sweetheart.

His parents had difficulties and eventually divorced. His father returned to Iowa. His mother and my mother became close friends for the remainder of their lives.

Brad and I lost touch over the years, and I didn't see him again until our tenth high school reunion. I missed the twentieth reunion. The last time I saw him was at the twenty-fifth reunion. We thoroughly enjoyed reminiscing about our youth and the adventures we shared. It seemed long ago, and it was. We mentioned things that the other had forgotten.

As class president, he spoke to the attendees prior to the band's start. Former members of the Soul Sanction reunited to play at the reunion, which made the evening perfect. Brad lost his speaking touch over the years and struggled through off-the-cuff remarks. He said it was nice to see everyone again, thanked them for coming, and wished them a wonderful and fun night.

My years as an undergraduate at Tennessee were four of the best years of my life. I carried my heavy involvement from high school into college. I proved my earlier prediction wrong and joined a fraternity. I was involved in several campus activities, including All Sing, Homecoming, and Carnicus (a combination of a carnival and a circus). I joined the Student Government Association and wrote a column for the student newspaper, *The Daily Beacon*.

I graduated with a journalism degree and accepted a position at *The Commercial Appeal* in Memphis. The country had suffered through the Watergate hearings, and every aspiring journalist wanted to be like Carl Bernstein and Bob Woodward, authors of *All the President's Men*. Journalism jobs were few and salaries were low. I realized that to advance in the newspaper business, an additional degree would help me progress. Following a five-year stint at the newspaper, I enrolled at Indiana University and earned a master's degree in journalism. I met my wife in Bloomington. Following graduation, I accepted a position at *The Tennessean* in Nashville. My roots were in Tennessee, and all roads eventually led back to the Volunteer State.

My mother called a few weeks ago and informed me that Brad decided to resume his favorite hobby of skydiving he learned as a paratrooper in the service. He made several jumps and joined an excursion with a group of veterans and friends with whom he formed a skydiving club.

The day was overcast with heavy winds. Evidently, some members of the group attempted to persuade Brad and another member from jumping, but they insisted. Brad continued his daredevil ways. His friends watched as Brad shot a thumbs up, and the plane departed the runway and disappeared into the dark gray heavens.

The group on the ground heard the plane's engine sputter and fight for life. They knew it was in trouble. They could not see the plane but heard the struggling cough of its engine. They prayed for its revival.

Silence. The men stood speechless, their necks straining with pain. Seconds seemed like hours. They prayed in vain to see the colorful barrage of parachutes breaking through the clouds.

The plane dropped with the grace of a swan in flight across a frozen Winter's lake. It did not spin nor turn but fell direct to meet its destiny in becoming one with the earth. We'll never know why Brad didn't parachute when the plane ran into trouble.

It was too difficult to explain my history with Brad to my wife. I told her that a friend from my youth had died, and I planned to attend the funeral in Knoxville. I wanted to attend to say goodbye, but mainly to say thanks.

The funeral resembled a high school reunion. Following the burial at the cemetery, the guests gathered at the church social hall. There were graduates from our class as well as others. Several veterans with whom Brad served attended the military service and reception.

The first person I encountered upon entering the room was my dear childhood friend, Sue Davis. I spoke to her briefly at the funeral and had the opportunity to catch up further at the reception. We recalled the disastrous New Year's Eve party at her house. I spoke to her the next day after the party, and she assured me that her parents weren't upset because the party crashers weren't invited. Even though I asked Brad to not call her, he did, she admitted, and said she was touched at how apologetic he was.

The biggest surprise was seeing Terry Dorcey again. We hadn't seen each other since our freshman year in college when we were assigned different residence halls and went our separate ways. After graduating from Tennessee, he attended Notre Dame Law School and became a successful attorney in Knoxville. More than any of my friends, he spent the most time with Brad and me. We reminisced about the Costa Rica trip and how helpful Brad had been in the rain forest. He mentioned how Brad assisted at the Boy Scout camp and saved a Scout's life. He said that of all his encounters with Brad, however, he was most impressed with his interaction with the boys at the psychiatric hospital.

"He was so patient and helpful with the kids," Terry said. "There were many Key Club members who were afraid to go to the hospital, and Brad wasn't in Key Club and volunteered several times. That one kid with the stutter really took to him."

"That was Ricky," I replied.

Terry couldn't end the conversation without one last dig at me. "Have you had any lime daiquiris lately?" I laughed and lied that it is my favorite happy hour beverage.

My heart sank, yet filled with excitement, when I spotted Sandy Channing. I walked to her, and we hugged. I thanked her for being there.

"When I read about Brad in the newspaper, I knew you would be here, and I wanted to personally extend my condolences. I know how much he meant to you, and I am so sorry," she said, touching my hand.

"We had many good times together," I noted, my voice cracking. "Several of them we never shared with anyone. We made many promises to each other." I laughed, and my mind briefly recalled the prostitute in Dallas.

Sandy and I briefed each other on our lives, and neither mentioned Skip.

I barely recognized Robbie Vandergriff when he joined me. He gained much weight and had gone bald since I last saw him in high school. He shook my hand and said, "Hey, wimp. How's it going?"

"Great," I replied. "I live and work in Nashville now."

"Remember our crazy times in Gatlinburg? I would have killed you had it not been for Brad. Sorry I was such a dick."

"How could I forget that experience?" I didn't want to discuss our poor relationship that developed. "It was an unforgettable Summer. Carefree life in the mountains. I wish life was as simple now."

"You and me both," he sighed and shook his head. "Too bad about Brad. He deserved better. Surviving Vietnam and all."

I nodded in agreement but didn't have a comment. We seemed to struggle for conversation. Another of Brad's Kings brothers, Randy Thomas, joined us and shook our hands.

"Too bad we see each other only on these occasions," Randy said. "It's a sign that we're getting older. Seems like only yesterday you and Brad went to Tennessee Tech with me and got wasted at that fraternity party."

"Don't remind me," I laughed. "I thought we were

going to get arrested."

"I ended up going to Tech and joined that fraternity. Small world," Randy said.

"Yes, it is," I replied with little interest.

It was difficult to recognize some of the guests I'd known in high school, but I saw Ron Johnson across the room and excused myself to join him.

"Ron Johnson, how the hell are you?" I said, slapping him on the back. He turned and immediately embraced me in a bear hug. I hoped my quitting the Royals had disappeared from his memory. He informed me that he remained in Knoxville and became a Knox County sheriff's deputy.

"It's good to see you," he said. "So sorry about Brad. I couldn't believe it."

"Yeah, it hit hard," I sighed.

"He was a great guy. I'll never forget how he saved our asses after initiation and gave us a ride home."

"Yeah, that was one of the worst experiences of my life. To this day I can't believe we went through that crap."

"You were right all along, Steve. We should have listened to you. Eventually all the clubs died out. They ceased to have a purpose. They're lucky they never killed anyone."

Several Kings and former athletes filled the room. They came to celebrate a life and not to be depressed. I was pleased to see so many of our high school friends.

We shared the best memories of our life together; the California trip and almost getting arrested in Mexico, Boy Scout camp, the MLK memorial service, the Billy Graham crusade, Costa Rica, Gatlinburg, and many others. Brad always thanked me for the opportunities I provided for him, but at the top of my list was our campaign and victory as senior class president and vice president. That was the Super Glue for our friendship. Brad taught me the facts of life and helped to make me the person I've become. He was my best friend.

One of my favorite movies is *Stand by Me*, based on Stephen King's novella, *The Body*. As the film concludes, narrator Gordie Lachance's final line is, "I never had any friends later on like the ones I had when I was 12. Jesus, does anyone?"

No.

About the Author

Larry Lunsford is a retired university administrator. He is co-author of *The First Year: Making the Most of College*, contributor to several collegiate first year student textbooks, contributing author to higher education books and publications, and has written hundreds of magazine and newspaper articles in his lengthy career. A native of Tennessee, he lives in Miami with his wife. *Brad* is his first novel. More information can be found at www.lwlunsford.com.

Made in the USA
Columbia, SC
24 October 2021